THE VAMPIRE HEIR

RITE WORLD 1: RITE OF THE VAMPIRE

JULIANA HAYGERT

COPYRIGHT

AUTHOR'S NOTE

I hope you enjoy reading *The Vampire Heir*!

Don't forget to sign up for my Newsletter to find out about new releases, cover reveals, giveaways, and more!

If you want to see exclusive teasers, help me decide on covers, read excerpts, talk about books, etc, join my reader group on Facebook: Juliana's Club!

RITE WORLD

Welcome to the RITE WORLD!

1

THEA

I was here. I couldn't believe it. I had made it.

Around me, the other ninety-nine people took over half the town square. While we waited for the train to come pick us up, they chatted and laughed and speculated how it would be, what we would see, who we would meet.

It was not every day Castle DuMoir opened its doors to the public. In fact, it only happened twice a year, and only one hundred lucky guests were invited randomly from the thousands, millions of requests they received.

And I was one of the lucky ones.

"Isn't this exciting?" a girl beside me asked. A wide smile adorned her lips as she bounced on the balls of her feet. Her excitement was irritating, if not saddening. "I can't believe I was chosen."

"Exciting," I said, though that couldn't be further from what I was feeling. If I stopped to think about this, if I considered all that could happen, that *would* happen ... I inhaled deeply, calming my racing heart, willing the shaking of my arms to stop.

"Oh." She reached over and squeezed my arm. "I see the train coming." She turned to me, her smile even wider than a few seconds ago, her brown eyes twinkling in the late afternoon sun.

The majestic, shiny black train slowed to a stop beside the small wooden platform that served as a station on the corner of the town's square. The glass doors opened, and a tall, handsome man wearing a black suit and a burgundy tie stepped out under the wide, dark awning covering the platform. There was a silver cross brooch on his lapel—the symbol of Castle DuMoir.

"Good evening, ladies and gentlemen," he said, his loud voice carrying over the crowd, shushing the guests. He grinned at us, which made his features even more handsome. "I'm Karl, your host for tonight's adventure. I have one question for you. Are you ready for the best night of your lives?" The crowd cheered. "Then, please, come on in. Have your invitation handy, as I'll need to check it before you come onboard the DuMoir train."

The guests hurried toward the train, pushing one another, trying to get in right away, as if the train would depart and leave them behind. Like a bouncer at a popular nightclub, Karl stood beside the door, making sure everyone who came through showed him their invitation.

The girl, still beside me, squealed as we approached the doors. "This is it. So exciting."

She stopped in front of Karl and flashed her invitation. Karl nodded at her. "Please, come in, young lady."

Then I was in front of him. The man was taller up close, harder, more imposing. But his smile didn't touch his blue eyes. I held his stare as I handed him my invitation, willing my hand not to shake. He plucked the beige paper from my hands and glanced at it. "Thea Harrington?"

I lifted my chin. "That's me."

He narrowed his eyes, but I refused to break under his gaze. This was just starting ... I wouldn't break down now.

The penny-sized brooch hidden in the inside pocket of my jacket trembled as he scrunched his nose and leaned away from me.

Karl tsked and returned the invitation to me, as if he was suddenly bored. "Welcome aboard, miss." He gestured to the doors.

"Thank you," I muttered, turning away from him.

A long, relieved breath escaped my lungs as I stepped inside the train.

The locomotive was even fancier on the inside. The darkened windows were large and curved upward, taking up most of the ceiling. Two columns of large, black leather armchairs stood on each side of the wide corridor, with touchscreen TVs and folding tables on their backs. Some chairs were turned backward, and a smooth wooden table stood between two rows.

From the magazines and articles I had read about the DuMoir visit, I knew there would also be a luxurious dining car, a movie theater car, a car with a pool, and even sleeping quarters.

I had started walking down the first car, when a hand grabbed my wrist. "Hey, sit here," the girl from before said, tugging on my arm gently.

I held in a grimace. This was not the time to make friends. I looked around, but the seats were filling up fast, and what would be my excuse to her? She had already seen I was as alone as she was.

I sighed. "Sure." I plopped down on the seat beside her.

She offered me her slender hand. "I'm Judy."

"Thea." I looked at her once more as I shook her hand firmly. She was probably my age, nineteen or maybe twenty, and she was pretty with auburn hair and tanned skin. I pulled my hand from hers and settled into my seat, looking straight ahead.

The girl, though, didn't seem to get the hint. "So, how long have you been trying to visit DuMoir?"

I suppressed a groan. "Two years."

"Oh, you're lucky."

I frowned. Was I? "They don't allow visitors younger than fifteen."

"True, but my entire family has been trying for years, and finally, I got the invitation." She tilted her head. "So, why do you want to see Castle DuMoir?"

The golden question. Everyone who was granted an invitation was asked that question. I clasped my hands together on my lap, glad I was shaking less and less, and told her what I had rehearsed for months now. "I've lived one town over for most of my life. There's nothing interesting around here, except the fact that there's a mysterious castle close by. Who doesn't want to see it? To know the faces of the lords and nobles living inside it?"

Her grin was so big, I thought it would blind me. "Exactly! I don't live in Crimson Glen, but my grandparents do. My parents were raised here until they got married and moved away, but we visit often. I've always dreamed of seeing the castle in person, to meet a prince, or a lord, or a royal guard, and ..." Her cheeks gained a red tint, and she quickly averted her gaze.

Holy crap, this girl thought she was headed straight to a fairy tale. Cinderella going to meet the prince at the ball. Poor girl.

My anxiety and nervousness were replaced by a white-hot anger. Anger for this girl and her dreams. "Well, anything can happen," I forced out.

She returned her eyes to mine, a small smile on her closed lips. "Anyway, I'm here to have a fun evening. I heard there's a village outside the castle with actual taverns and inns and stables, like old stuff, you know?"

I nodded. "There's also a lake and boat rides, and a small winery."

"And to crown the night, a tour inside the castle and a masquerade party in the ballroom."

A chill went down my spine. "That's right."

"So exciting," Judy repeated for the tenth time or so. If I had to guess, I would hear that same tone coming from her at least another five hundred times until the end of this visit.

When the passengers were seated and the doors closed, Karl's voice rang through the speakers. "Welcome aboard, ladies and gentlemen. Please, make yourself comfortable. Fun fact about our fabulous train: It can hit 250 miles per hour, but because DuMoir is only forty miles away and the scenery is beautiful at sunset, we'll take this trip slow."

A beautiful woman in a black suit, burgundy shirt, and the silver cross pin appeared by my side. With a wide smile, she unfolded each of our tables, depositing on them crystal flutes filled with bubbling liquid.

"Thanks," I whispered as she turned around and served the guests on the other side of the corridor.

"Please, enjoy a glass of one of our finest wines, produced

at the DuMoir estate," Karl continued. "If you need anything, our attendants can certainly help you. Enjoy the ride. We'll be at the DuMoir Castle in less than thirty minutes."

I eyed the flute and the champagne-like liquid in front of me.

I swallowed hard.

Beside me, Judy downed her champagne in one big gulp. With a loud, "Aahh," she set down her glass and turned to me. "It's delicious. Drink it."

From the corner of my eye, I glanced at the attendants nearby. "I don't really drink this kind of stuff."

"But it's great. You'll like it."

"No, I don't want it."

"Why not? We're here to enjoy this visit. Here's the first taste."

I scrunched my nose. "I'm not—"

Judy exhaled. "Fine, then I'll drink it." I gasped as she grabbed my flute and drank the entire thing in less than two seconds. My throat went dry and my heart sped up. Again, I glanced at the attendants, this time not so discreet, but none of them were looking at us. Thankfully, Judy placed my now empty glass in front of me again. "Well, that was even better the second time around." She chuckled.

"You have no idea what you've done," I whispered, wishing she wouldn't really hear me.

She shrugged. "This fancy trip is free. I'm eating and drinking and taking everything they hand me. And if you don't want it, I'll have yours too." She grinned, still looking as innocent and cheerful as the girl who first talked to me in the town's square not twenty minutes ago.

My fingers itched, and even though I didn't know this girl,

a sudden urge to reach out and hold her hand assaulted me, too strong to contain. A small gasp escaped through my lips, but instead of reaching for her, I sat on my hands and looked straight ahead, eager for this night to be over.

For this whole thing to be over.

2

DRAKE

AFTER THIRTEEN DAYS OF INCESSANT FIGHTING, MY EXHAUSTION ran bone-deep.

Every step on the wide, shiny black staircase took more effort than I cared to admit.

I passed three human servants, who stared at my bloodied armor for one second too long before remembering their place and bowing deeply as I walked by.

I groaned. This place was crawling with humans.

Two men dressed in the castle's colors—black suit and deep red tie—stood in front of the double doors of Reynard's office. They didn't even look at me as I approached. They simply opened the doors, and I stepped aside.

"Drake." Reynard's voice floated toward me before I could place him. *Them.*

Though the room was filled with Reynard's poignant scent, as I walked into the room, I smelled Alex's presence, too.

With a glass of red liquid in his hand, Reynard poked his blond head around the corner of his office. "We're in here." I marched toward the long mahogany table and black leather armchairs, which sat before the large glass windows, then turned to the right. The office opened into a larger entertainment room, complete with pool table, low sofas, a big screen, and movie theater-like chairs. A bar stood against one wall crammed full of alcohol and blood.

Reynard stood between the pool table and the bar, sipping from his drink, while Alex leaned over the pool table, his mop of brown hair falling over his shoulders and face as he made a move. His cue stick hit the white ball with precision, and he pocketed four balls.

With a cat's grin, Alex straightened and stared at me. "Hello, Drake. How were the northern mountains?"

I reined in my hate for the insufferable prick and offered him the same predator's smile. "Cold and distant." Then, I turned to Reynard, our leader, and started on my report. "I tried solving the werewolves' problems peacefully, but they weren't having it. A battle ensued, and after thirteen days of fighting nonstop, I finally broke through. I killed their leaders, rounded the rest of the pack up, picked new leaders, and explained the rules to everyone." I gestured down my bloodied armor. "I just got back."

Reynard glanced at my clothes and clicked his tongue. "You should have rested before coming to me."

"I can rest later," I assured him. "Now, I just want a meal and a warm bath."

"Oh, you're hungry?" Alex asked, his voice amused. "Brianna, come here, darling." As if pulled by a string, a young woman in a skimpy white dress appeared from behind the couch. She stood and I closed my eyes for a moment as if it hurt to look at such a young, pretty girl with several crusted over wounds on her once unmarred neck. Like a doll, she strolled toward Alex. "Take a bite," he offered.

I suppressed a growl, though I was sure he could hear it rumbling inside my chest. "No, thank you," I hissed.

He shook his head once. "Well, if you won't have it ..." He wound his arm around the young woman's waist, pulled her close, and holding my gaze, he bared his teeth. His canines elongated, then he bit down on her neck.

The girl gasped in pleasure. The poor thing was probably a junkie, used to being a blood bag, used to our ecstasy-inducing saliva. A vampire's bite was as addicting as it was dangerous.

Blood trickled down her neck, into the deep cleavage of her dress, between her plump breasts.

My mouth watered.

"Alex, you should put that blood slave out of her misery sooner rather than later," Reynard barked, watching as Alex drank the girl's blood with gusto. Reynard shook his head once, then turned to the bar. There, he picked one of many bottles filled with fresh blood and filled a fat glass to the brim. He offered it to me.

"Thank you," I muttered, taking the glass. I inhaled deeply, letting the metallic heavy scent fill my senses. Then, I gulped it down as if there was a fire inside me and this drink, this red liquid, was the only thing that could quench it.

"There," Alex said, letting go of the girl. Her body slumped to the floor like a potato sack. Like a real prince, Alex picked a handkerchief out of his suit's pocket and cleaned his mouth. As for the girl, he didn't even glance at her again. "I'll have someone dispose of the body."

Reynard ignored him and said to me, "That pack has been giving us trouble for years." He absently reached for the silver cross pendant hanging over his shirt and twisted it between his thumb and index finger, as he usually did whenever he was thinking too hard.

I had been sent up there, to the northern, colder parts of Canada, to deal with it more times than I liked to remember. The crazy alpha had risen into power by sheer luck, and he resented the fact that his kind should remain hidden, should abide by rules. In one of his rage episodes, the alpha had led a team to decimate a small human village because some children decided to play in the forest and crossed into their territory by accident. Another time, vampires—good friends of Reynard—had been in the area visiting acquaintances. Apparently, one vampire got into a beef with a werewolf at a local bar, and the entire pack turned on the vampires. Usually, one to one, it was hard to tell who would win—it depended on the age of the vampire and the size of the werewolf, but dozens of werewolves against a handful of unprepared vampires? Not a chance.

Then rumors arrived that the alpha had been planning to round up other packs—they wanted an all-out war with the humans. If that were his plan, he needed to be stopped, and as the most powerful group of supernaturals on this side of the globe, we had to deal with him. And so, as one of the princes—a nickname for the few hand-chosen vampires Reynard trusted, the ones in the line of succession in case Reynard abdicated—I was sent to find out what was going on and solve it. In the end, the rumors were true, and the alpha had aligned with three other packs. In fact, the day I arrived, they attacked another village nearby. I wasn't able to save those humans, but after days of fighting, I had put an end to that crazy plan.

Or so I hoped.

"It should be all solved now," I said. The poor girl's body on the floor felt like a magnet, but I fought against the pull and didn't look at it.

"Great." Reynard patted my shoulder twice. "You know I'll want all the details, but you should go clean up. You have one hour to rest." I lifted an eyebrow at him. "You forgot?"

Then it hit me. The bi-annual tour. It was today. Later tonight. Damn. I had stayed away for so long, I had forgotten.

"There's too much on my mind," I explained.

Alex snorted. "It's the biggest event, and you forgot?"

Reynard went on, again ignoring Alex. "I'll see you in the ballroom in an hour."

I bowed my head. "Yes, my Lord."

Reynard, with his appearance of late thirties, but with too many years on his back, practically rolled his eyes at me. "Don't call me that." He waved me off. "Now get ready for our feast."

3

THEA

I THOUGHT I HAD PREPARED MYSELF BEFORE COMING HERE. I had read all the articles, seen all the published pictures, read interviews with people who worked for and with the castle's habitants. I had even researched Lord Reynard and his princes—his many adopted sons—and how long ago his ancestors had come from Europe and helped shape the United States' history.

But nothing could have prepared me for the real Castle DuMoir. Nothing could have prepared me for how magical and beautiful and unreal this place looked and felt.

The village was straight out of the 1800s, but well-kept and with electric lamps illuminating the stone paved roads. The lake made a thick C around the village, and its banks were white sand, torches lit every few feet, and the water was pitch black shining under the moonlight. When it was time for the boat ride, the guests were divided into five smaller groups and each boarded a luxurious yacht. The winery was a maze of tall hedges that always ended in some kind of plaza

—one had stone benches, another had a small fountain, another had a little chapel, and more.

All the while, they offered us food and drink—a taste of stew and ale at the tavern, champagne and hors d'oeuvres in one of the yachts, grapes and cheese and wine at the winery. I confess I tasted them all, but I never took more than half a bite. Meanwhile, Judy ate her part and mine and always asked for more.

I was careful when letting her finish my portions, watching out so Karl and his convoy weren't looking at us. I didn't think they saw it.

When our group was finally being guided from the village to the castle through a long, winding, uphill trail, Judy frowned at me. "Did you notice all the people we encountered here are too beautiful?" The light coming from the lamps flanking the path illuminated half her face.

"Yes," I answered. There was no reason to lie.

"Seriously, it's like that's a requirement to work here. The job application probably says something like 'you should be me more beautiful than a Greek god or goddess.'" She chuckled at her own joke. "That's the only thing I can think of."

"Maybe it's luck," I said. But it wasn't luck, it was consequence. And it wasn't only the people serving in the stores or restaurants. The many guards positioned throughout the estate were also as attractive as Karl and his assistants.

"I want to be lucky like this," she whispered.

You have no idea what you're talking about, I wanted to tell her, but I kept my mouth shut.

So far, I had been able to keep the anxiety at bay and almost enjoy this visit. Almost.

But, as we rounded the last curve of the path, and it

opened to a big clearing, which was probably a beautiful, colorful garden when in the sunlight, revealing the large stone castle with its turrets and balconies and its many illuminated windows, my heart skipped a beat.

The anxiety and nervousness slammed back into my chest. After a sharp inhale, my heartbeat sped up, and I rubbed my clammy palms on my jeans.

"It's so pretty," Judy said, her tone carrying a dreamy lilt. "So grand, so imposing." She sighed as if being here, seeing this castle was the biggest achievement of her life. "I bet it's even prettier during the day."

Karl guided us down another stone path that cut through the garden and led us straight to the castle's front entrance. Wide stone stairs led up to huge dark wooden doors—the doors alone were sixteen or seventeen feet tall.

Karl gestured for us to stop, then raced up the stairs and faced us with a big grin. "Ladies and gentlemen. We'll now walk around some of the most beautiful rooms of the castle, like the foyer, the living room, the library, the dining room, and after changing into ball attire, we'll finally stop at the ballroom, where we'll meet the other groups and party before it all ends." I sucked in a sharp breath. Wary, I glanced around, but everyone was still smiling, still laughing, still content about the visit. "Who knows? We might see Lord Reynard or a prince or two around the corridors." Some women, including Judy, let out sounds like shrieks of anticipation. "Please, follow me."

Like a good guide, Karl led us through the castle, telling us interesting facts about each room, like where the materials used in the foyer's construction came from, which books Lord Reynard treasured the most in the library, who was who in the many paintings spread along the hallway walls, the many illustrious guests that Lord Reynard, and his ancestors before him, entertained in the living room, which instruments Lord Reynard knew how to play in the music room, and which was Lord Reynard's favorite food in the dining room—the table was covered with these rare dishes, and the guests were invited to try them out.

As usual, Judy ate all that crossed her path. I approached the table, pretended to pick at a bruschetta, but didn't eat anything. By now, Judy and the guests were starting to trip over their own feet.

Then, finally, we were taken to large rooms with vanities, chairs, mirrors, and hangers filled with luscious gowns. A couple of young women met us at the doors and guided us to the vanities where they styled our hair and enhanced our makeup. The girl helping me chose a long, full black gown for me. When I reluctantly put it on, I felt awkward and out of place. I was used to fancy dresses and attire, but it didn't seem like a good idea to be dressed like this here. I especially didn't like the way the dress exposed my neck and shoulders—I shuddered.

Next, they took us back to a wide hallway, and at the end, I could see a grand, curved archway in smooth, white stone.

I barely had time to acknowledge the beauty of the ballroom as we crossed beneath the archway and stepped inside. Two young women, standing to the side of the archway, handed us champagne flutes.

"Please, join us in the center," one of them said. "Lord Reynard will make an appearance soon."

This was it. It was almost time. I inhaled sharply as the anxiety returned in full force.

"Wow," Judy muttered, her huge eyes going from the young woman's face, to the champagne in her hand, to the ballroom. She had a dark green gown on, which went well with her smooth skin and brown hair.

I tried shoving my nervousness to the back of my mind and live in the moment. Pretending I was fine, I took in the room.

Wow indeed.

Our shoes made a *clink-clink* sound on the shiny, black stone floor as we walked deeper into the large, white-walled ballroom. I looked around and felt like an ant in the imposing room. The ceiling was five stories high, and right in the center, it curved downward as if the weight of the three big, crystal chandeliers were too much to bear. Floor-to-ceiling windows took up most of south side of the room, and on the north side, a wide staircase led to a large balcony with a black, stone railing.

One hundred people in this ballroom was nothing, and we all huddled in the center, admiring the place.

"What now?" I heard a woman to my right ask the man beside her. Looking like a politician in his sleek tuxedo, the man simply shrugged.

I glanced around. Everyone was chatting, grinning, admiring the place, enjoying their fine clothes, and sipping their champagne.

"You won't even drink that one?" Judy asked me, her eyes huge, as if I were absolutely crazy. "Give it to me, then." She reached for my flute, but I pulled it back.

"No, let me keep this one." This one ... this one they would be watching closely.

She recoiled, hurt by my barked words. "Oh-kay."

Karl appeared on the stairs. With graceful steps, he went up to the balcony then smiled down at us. "Ladies and gentlemen, it's my pleasure to introduce you to the owner of this beautiful castle, Lord Reynard DuMoir."

The doors at the back of the balcony opened and a tall man with long, blond hair emerged from the shadows to loom over us at the balcony railing. He wore an elegant black tux with black shirt and burgundy tie and a long, black cape. His smile was even more dazzling than Karl's.

Ten young men trailed behind him, all dressed in the same black tux but with white shirts and without the dramatic cape. The men formed a half circle around the lord of the castle.

The princes.

The glass felt slippery in my damp hands. I let out a shuddering breath.

"Oh my God," Judy whispered beside me. "They are all … gorgeous!"

Indeed, like everyone in this castle, the young princes were all handsome in a too-perfect-to-be-true way.

"Welcome to my little castle," Lord Reynard said, his rough voice booming all around us. "I'm so glad you are here tonight. Please, let's celebrate." The two young women who had been distributing drinks at the doors a few moments ago, now walked among the princes and Lord Reynard, handing out silver flutes. I wondered if they really had champagne in those. Lord Reynard took a flute, then raised it high. "To a happy night."

Ninety-nine guests smiled at him. Ninety-nine guests lifted their glasses to the lord of the castle. Ninety-nine guests downed their champagne in two, three gulps.

I quickly put the rim of the glass to my lips, but drank only a sip, then as if I had choked on the drink, I lowered my head and coughed, while not so subtly dumping the rest of my champagne on the floor.

Ninety-nine guests swayed and barely paid any attention as Lord Reynard and the princes discarded their flutes. Ninety-nine guests swayed and didn't even noticed as the other six doors on the bottom floor of the ballroom opened and more incredibly beautiful people, mostly men, entered the room and lined the walls. Ninety-nine guests didn't see as the doors were closed again and locked.

My heart thundered in my chest. The glass finally slipped from my trembling hand and shattered on the floor.

"My dear guests," Lord Reynard said, knowing the guests couldn't really make out his words anymore, not ninety-nine of them at least. Though I was sure his speech was part of the game. Part of the thrill. "I'm so, *so* glad you are here tonight. You see, we only have theses feasts twice a year so as not to attract unwanted attention. Do you know how much work is involved in making sure you all disappear and no one comes looking for you?" He took a step down the stairs. "If it was a little easier, we would do it more often, because, oh, we almost starve between these parties." He took another step down. "Almost."

Judy bumped into me and I nearly jumped out of my skin. I grabbed her arm and turned her to me. Her eyes were dazed and her mouth hung open, like she wanted to smile, but her jaw was too numb. Damn, I should have stopped her from drinking and eating.

"Judy," I whispered her name, trying to shake her off the induced stupor.

Lord Reynard took another step down the stairs. "Now, my dear guests, I want to thank you for coming. For sending your request to visit us and for accepting our invitation."

In rhythm with Lord Reynard, the people along the walls advanced forward a foot.

No, I shouldn't have stopped Judy from drinking and eating. Maybe *I* should have drank and eaten a little more, then my heart wouldn't be thumping so hard against my chest, it hurt.

I inhaled deeply, trying to slow my breathing, to calm my heart, before one of them noticed—*heard*—I wasn't a freaking doll like the others.

Lord Reynard grinned, revealing his fangs. "Thank you, my guests, for your generous donation." Like a cat, he leaped from the stairs. I watched, my heart skipping a beat, as he seemed to float in the air for two seconds, making a graceful arc above our heads. Then, he landed silently in the middle of the guests. I held in a gasp, but the other ninety-nine guests didn't even blink. "Let's feast!" he yelled.

The vampires attacked.

4

DRAKE

THE FEAST HAPPENED TWICE A YEAR, BUT BY THE WAY THE others advanced on the humans, it seemed we only invited them here once every decade.

Reynard was the first to sink his teeth in the shiny skin of a young woman. The moment he took the first gulp, the other princes were all over the ballroom, taking their own victims. Only then did the other vampires around the perimeter of the room go in for their meal.

I stayed on the balcony, watching the horrors below me as the heavy scent of blood infected the air. Too sweet, too alluring. I closed my eyes, fisted my hands, and held my ground.

I hadn't been human for many years, but I still remembered how easily they got scared, how they held on to fear. Fear had been stripped away from the one hundred guests by all the drinks offered while on the estate. The last glass of champagne they drank was laced with the final touch, one last drop of elixir to make them compliant. Only a handful of the guests were resistant, but they were still drunk on it and couldn't run or do anything other than scream while the vampires came for them.

The guests weren't randomly chosen. Besides not having a large family we needed to worry about, they were picked based on Reynard's and the princes' preferences.

Cain was probably the least picky one. As long as blood was flowing down his throat, he didn't care. Nolan, Aston, and Gray went for the big guys—men in their thirties, forties, who were strong enough to put up a fight if they weren't affected by the elixir. They liked a good brawl. Alex, Patrick, and Phelps always chose girls around our human ages—from twenty to twenty-five—so they could rub themselves all over them while draining them of blood. I didn't know what sickened me more. To watch that or Dorian and Albert while they fed on the little ones, the fifteen year olds. According to them, the youngest had the freshest, sweetest blood of all.

I couldn't understand how Reynard allowed children to be brought to the castle. If it were up to me, we would only allow people over twenty-one in here.

But I was not the lord of the castle.

And if Dorian and Alex had their way, I would never be.

Even through the enticing blood, her spicy and earthy scent hit my nostrils, and I turned to the door behind me as she walked into the ballroom.

A small smile tugged on my lips. "Sarki."

The oracle, a beautiful woman with long, black curls and smooth, dark skin, strolled to me, her brown eyes on the carnage below. The skirt of her dark red robe brushed against the black floor, hiding her feet. She looked more like a priestess ready for a sacred ritual than an ancient being ready for the feast.

Sarki halted by my side. "Hello, young Drake."

My grin widened. Only she would call a five-hundred-year-old vampire young. "Came to join the fun?"

She snorted. "Fun? This is ridiculous. And I know you feel the same."

A crease settled between my brows. "Have you ever tried to stop this?"

"Reynard only listens to me when it's convenient for him."

I nodded, knowing what she meant. But maybe someday it would change. I didn't like to think that someday Reynard wouldn't be among us all. After all, he was a father to me, and despite all of his flaws, I cared for him as such, but he was the one who had instilled the princes' rank several hundred years ago and chosen the ones he found were the best to succeed him in case something happened to him. As he always said, we lived in a dangerous world, and dealing with supernaturals was always a risk. We had already lost too many good friends over the centuries.

However, in the event of Reynard's death, I wished one of the good princes would take his place.

I didn't like thinking what would happen if Alex or Dorian ended up as lord of the castle. These feasts would become a monthly occurrence, the number of guests would double, and there wouldn't be an age limit. I grimaced.

In one fast movement, the oracle reached for me and took my hand in hers, squeezing hard. "Sarki?"

A white shadow fell over her eyes, and she stared straight ahead, seeing nothing and everything. "It has arrived. It's here," she said in the eerie voice she got whenever she was having a vision. "It has come."

"What? What has come?"

"The missing piece holding our salvation." She turned those milky eyes to me. "Your salvation. Find the new and unite it with the old." Sarki blinked. Her eyes returned to normal. "Wasn't that mysterious?" she joked, letting go of my hand.

"What did you see?"

She shook her head once. "Not much. I never see much. I just get a feeling." She placed a hand over her chest. "I don't know what that meant."

With that, she walked off to the side of the balcony. I stared after her, wondering how strange it must be, to get visions, feelings, and not know what to do with them. Reynard, though, he always dug until he found a meaning. If he didn't find one, he created one.

But this was the first time in the almost five hundred years I had been with Reynard and Sarki that she had talked to me when foretelling something. First time it was for me.

Distracted by these thoughts, I only sensed the new presence two seconds in advance. My head snapped to the side as a woman came rushing up the stairs and threw herself at me.

"Please, help me," she rasped between sobs. "Please, save me."

I froze.

Her arms were warm around my waist and her scent ... I tried not to breathe, but it was impossible. There was blood smeared all over her clothes. I had no idea if it was hers or someone else's. At this point, my brain didn't care anymore.

She pulled back and looked up at me with big, brown eyes. "Please, sir, help me."

Why she had come to me, I had no idea. Perhaps because I was the only one away from the massacre? The only one not dirty with blood, with my teeth still retracted?

But temptation was right here, facing me with desperation on her face.

I had been so, so good. I could endure a little longer—

She turned her face to the floor below, exposing her pretty little neck to me. She let out a cry. "Can't you see? It's madness."

Oh, I could see it. I could see the madness that the pulsing vein in her neck was driving me to. I could hear her blood rushing, her heart thumping.

My control snapped.

I sank my teeth into her neck.

Her deliciously warm blood flowed into my mouth and down my throat, and I practically purred in delight. Fresh blood was the best thing on this Earth. Every time I tasted it, I wondered why the hell I resisted it so much. Why did I prefer the bottled version? Not that it was much worse. Our servants put together the bottles from blood bags we got from hospitals and labs, or from draining the humans we kept alive during the feast, the blood slaves we saved for later.

Because I wasn't an animal.

I pushed the girl back before I drained her, disgusted with myself. If she hadn't been dazed with the elixir, she was dazed now, after having half her blood taken.

Gently, I helped her to the ground, and then sidestepped her, trying not to feel too guilty for something that was supposed to be natural for someone like me. Even after almost five hundred years, this never felt natural.

Wishing there was somewhere better I could hide the woman, I fished a handkerchief from my tux pocket and cleaned the corners of my mouth.

My gaze returned to the bloodbath below, looking for a distraction to occupy my mind before I finished what I had started. Right in the center of the ballroom, an unusual scene caught my attention. A young woman hugged another one tightly against her chest, trying to keep her upright, while dodging the blood-crazy vampires. Eden, one of Alex's guys, advanced on them, and she blocked his hands with her upper arm, and then landed a beautiful front snap kick right to his chest. The vampire stumbled back, only to bare his fangs at her.

In two seconds, I was standing between the young women and Eden.

"Leave them alone," I said without really thinking.

Eden snarled at me. "Are you laying claim on them, prince?"

Then, Alex, with his lips smeared with blood, was right beside Eden. "My man here was going for them before you, Drake." Alex looked at the young women, his eyes shining with lust and hunger. "Unless you intend to claim them, I'll have the blond one."

"And I'll have the redhead," Eden said, his voice too eager.

I glanced over my shoulder at the girls. The blond didn't seem affected by the elixir at all. She was holding the red-haired girl as if her life depended on it, while still aware of all that occurred around her. From her stance, I knew she was ready to land another nasty kick to whoever got too close.

Her light gray eyes met mine, despair stamped on them, and a chill ran down my spine.

I lifted my chin and faced Alex. "Yes, I'm claiming them." I pointed at the two young women and said louder, so everyone around us could hear me. "I lay claim on these two girls. They are mine."

5

THEA

I THOUGHT I WOULDN'T PANIC, BUT THE MOMENT THE VAMPS jumped us, my heart went through my throat and I realized I was so, so wrong.

I was not prepared for this.

The vamps took their first victims and I wanted to scream. People should be shrieking, they should be running, but they were too dazed, too high on whatever was in our drinks to do anything other than stand there and wait to be turned into a meal.

I had to act as such, too. I closed my eyes and inhaled deeply, trying to slow my racing heart.

My eyes snapped open when Judy huffed. A vampire had grabbed her. I should have let him do it; I should have let him kill her right then.

The vamp bit her neck. Judy moaned and became a limp mass in his arms.

I couldn't do it. I couldn't let them take her like that.

Abandoning all reason, I kicked the vampire in the hip, hard enough to get his attention, to make him release his mouth from her skin. He stared at me, fangs bared, and dropped Judy on the floor like a discarded soda can. Then, he came for me.

I stood my ground as the brooch, now tucked inside my cleavage, warmed enough to hurt my skin.

The vampire halted a foot from me and scrunched his nose. "What the hell?" He took a step back. "Your blood smells ... spoiled."

I ignored his comment and knelt beside my friend. "Judy." I brushed her hair from her face and lifted her head. "Wake up, Judy." She moaned in response. "Shit." With the little strength I had, I hooked my arms around her shoulders and hauled her up. "Please, help me," I said to her, but I knew she was too high on the elixir and the bite to carry her own weight.

Around us, the vamps feasted—drinking their victims' blood and feeling up their bodies. Nausea revolved in my stomach, and it was all I could do not to throw up.

I didn't know how much time had passed, but soon, most of the guests were pushed aside on the floor. And, in one corner, a few satisfied vamps rounded up humans—the blood slaves they were saving for later.

"Come on," I groaned at Judy, trying to pass her arm around my shoulders so it wouldn't be too hard to keep her upright. "We gotta go." I jerked my chin toward the cattle-like humans.

As I turned, hauling Judy with me, another vampire appeared right in front of me. "Hm, what do we have here?" He leaned closer, and like the other one, scrunched his nose at me. "What is wrong with you?" He sniffed once more, and probably catching the blood on her neck, his eyes landed on Judy. "She smells nice."

He reached for her.

Without thinking, I kicked him square in the chest, sending him back a couple of steps.

The vampire snarled at me, ready to rip my throat out.

Shit.

Then, another vampire—a prince—appeared out of nowhere between Judy and me and the enraged vamp. I felt like I was in a daze as a second prince showed up, and they discussed our fate. I wanted to butt in and say something, but what? My thundering heart and sweaty palms didn't help. I had to slip away and go to the corner with the other humans who would be kept alive.

I inhaled deeply, ready to sprint if I had to.

Until the prince looked over his shoulder at me. The moment his harsh green eyes met mine, I froze.

The prince—Drake, that was what they had called him—returned his gaze to the other two vampires. "Yes, I'm claiming them." He pointed at Judy and me, then said in a louder, steadier voice, "I lay claim on these two girls. They are mine."

What did he mean, we were his?

That filled me with frustration, and questions, but with the number of vampires closing in on us with their shiny, sharp fangs out, those questions would have to wait. At least this vamp, this prince, had his fangs hidden, and he was the only one who didn't seem smeared by blood and didn't have his clothes rumpled from tangling with the humans.

In my arms, Judy moaned again, still riding the high.

The other prince let out a hollow chuckle. "Typical. Prince Drake taking on the peasants."

Drake took a step back and stood by my side. "Do you have a problem with it, Prince Alex?"

Alex sported a sly grin. "Oh no, not at all."

After a showdown of testosterone, Drake turned to me. "Give me your friend." Even if he weren't a vampire, his height, the width of his shoulders, and the sheer power in his voice would have intimidated me. I only held Judy tighter. "If you want to live, I suggest you hand me your friend and come with me."

His green eyes looked so bright, so deep—too human. No, not human. This man was not human. I had to keep in mind that none of them were human. However, it didn't seem like my first plan would work. The cattle-like humans were on the other side of the room, and I knew, I knew the moment I stepped away from this prince, the others would be all over me. Perhaps they wouldn't want to drink my blood, but they could kill me with a snap of their fingers, and they could take Judy.

I didn't have many options here.

"Okay," I muttered, loosening my grip around Judy. Drake scooped her up as if she were nothing more than a rag doll.

Next, he took my hand and curled it around his elbow. "Stay with me," he said with a bark. An order.

With Judy secured in his arms, Drake guided me across the ballroom toward the staircase. He glanced up, to the side of the balcony, where a gorgeous woman with black hair and dark skin and an elegant burgundy robe stood, watching us with a tight smile on her lips.

The oracle.

I averted my eyes.

"W-where are you taking us?" I asked, afraid of his answer. For all I knew, he could simply take us both to another room, lock us in there, and feed on us.

"To safety." He glanced at me again. "I'm Drake. What's your name?"

I paused for a moment, wondering if I should tell him. I couldn't find any reason not to. "Thea."

He looked down to his arms. "And hers?"

"Judy." One vampire made a pass at me. Drake noticed and turned toward him, ready to strike or defend, I didn't know. But the moment the vampire smelled me, he snarled and retreated. Without wasting a second, Drake tugged at my arm, and we resumed marching across the ballroom. Wasn't he curious about why the others couldn't get close to me? I was curious as to why he could. "That other ... vampire," I paused, trying to pass surprise and incredulity when pronouncing the word as if I hadn't known until tonight vampires were real. "That vampire back there, he said my blood smelled spoiled to him. Isn't it the same with you?"

He halted at the base of the staircase and glanced at me again. "No. Your scent is ..." He sucked in a sharp breath, and then shook his head once. "Your blood smells fine. Just fine."

That was a surprise.

I opened my mouth to ask more—I had to understand how he was getting around it—but I swallowed a gasp instead.

The ballroom went dark.

My heart stopped for a moment, and a chill went down my spine as screams and loud bangs and rapid movement filled my ears. Drake's arm tensed under my hand. Something like a growl came from him. He moved forward, but my foot caught on the stair, and I fell on my knees. This time, I couldn't contain the yelp that ripped out from my chest.

I was in a dark room full of vampires.

Tears of despair and fear burned behind my eyelids. I was

blind here, but the vampires weren't, not completely. They couldn't see as well as if the lights were still on, but they could make out a few silhouettes and masses.

Fingering my surroundings, I stood and reached for Drake. Only to find an empty space where he had been a moment ago.

"D-drake?" I called quietly, afraid that someone else, another vampire, would hear me. Who was I kidding? I could whisper, and they all would hear it.

A heartbeat passed. "I'm here," Drake said, taking my hand in his. He tugged me close to him. "Just ... stay quiet."

I wanted to ask him what was happening, but the likelihood that he would answer me was low. Besides, I was afraid of the answer.

The lights flickered on.

I gasped in relief, and then I gasped in horror.

Along the perimeter of the room, half a dozen vampires were pinned to the walls by thick swords pierced through their shoulders, and thick wooden staves were driven through their chests.

My hands flew to my mouth.

Beside me, Drake sucked in a sharp breath. I followed his line of sight, and atop the stairs, I saw a seventh vampire nailed to the wall.

Drake rasped, "Lord Reynard."

I BLINKED ONCE, TWICE, THREE TIMES. BUT THE MAN WHO TOOK me in, who made me feel less disgusted about what I was, was now pinned to the wall, a stake deep in his heart.

My insides became fire, and rage swept over me. I turned around and shouted at the frozen people in the ballroom. "Who the hell did this?"

Alex, his eyes rimmed with red, was right in my face in a second. "Who says it wasn't you?" He glanced at Judy and Thea. "The human lover."

I fisted my hands, reining in my rage, willing myself to not rip his throat out right then. Hell knew I had wanted to do that since I first met him hundreds of years ago.

"That man was like a father to me."

Alex snorted. "Father. That's another human word. Vampires don't have fathers. We have allies, we have companions, we have partners, we have servants." Once more, he looked at the girls with me. "We have slaves."

I growled, advancing on him. Dorian's arm shot out to

stop me. "This is not the time," he said, his voice harsh. "The other vampires seem confused, and the remaining humans are waking up from their stupor. We need to do something. We can discuss other matters later."

I took a long breath. "You're right."

Alex didn't seem too convinced, but he nodded and stepped back.

"We should clear the room," Aston said, appearing beside us. "Starting with the humans." He, too, glanced at the girls.

"Then do it," I said, swallowing an exasperated sigh. "Take the humans to their place. I'll take care of these two and meet you here in a few minutes."

I didn't wait for their responses. I turned, and with Judy in my arms and Thea beside me, I marched out of the ballroom through one of the doors in the first floor.

Thea's rapid breathing and heartbeat told me she was scared and tired, but she held on and didn't question me. She simply followed close—too close, her sweet scent teasing me —while I took them through the wide corridors, up two flights of stairs, then through another winding corridor.

"Prince Drake," Thomas said, appearing around the corner. The young boy rushed toward us, his eyes wide. "What happened?"

"I don't have time to explain." I handed Judy to him. Thankfully, the boy was strong for a sixteen-year-old human and was able to pick the girl up easily. "Just take them to my quarters, put them in a spare bedroom, and keep them there. If you can, find the valerian salve from the infirmary and give it to this one." I jerked my chin to Judy. "I'll be back as soon as I can."

Thomas nodded. "Yes, prince."

Then, I turned to Thea. "Do not try to escape." I stared at her. To her credit, she didn't even flinch as I towered over her, over her delicate frame, and poured some of my anger into my features. "You won't get far if you try, and it'll only make things worse. In fact, I don't think I can save you again. Do you understand?"

She swallowed hard. "Yes," she said, her voice firm. She flipped her long blond hair aside, as if trying to prove she wasn't afraid. But her visibly shaking hand proved otherwise.

If chaos didn't wait for me in the ballroom, I would have never left her alone with Thomas in the castle's corridors. But I had no choice. Right now, I had to trust she would listen to me. Hopefully, she was still dazed from finding out vampires were real, and too scared by the gruesome deaths in the ballroom to try anything stupid.

Without another word, I rushed back downstairs to the ballroom.

The humans had already been cleared out, and the bodies of Reynard and six of his personal guards had been taken down from the walls. They had been placed side by side in the center of the ballroom.

The princes, the oracle, Reynard's consorts, and a few other members of the DuMoir house surrounded the dead. And around them, twelve vampire guards formed a loose ring —if to keep someone in or out, I wasn't sure yet.

"There he is," Alex said the moment I joined them. "Where were you when the lights were out?"

Everyone turned to me. I bit back a growl. "Escorting the young women out of the ballroom."

"Yes, of course." He clicked his tongue. "The human lover was stacking up more humans for his little side of the castle."

"That has nothing to do with what happened here," Nolan said. "Yes, we all know about Drake's particular tastes —" He gestured toward me as if I were a mere mortal. "—but we need to focus on the problem at hand."

Albert stared at Nolan. "And where were you when Reynard was killed?"

"That's nonsense," I muttered. All eyes fell on me. "We were all in the ballroom," I said louder. "Almost every vampire living in this state was in the ballroom when the lights went out. It could have been … any of us."

Alex clenched his fists. "What are you implying?"

I exhaled. "I'm not implying anything. I'm stating a fact."

Patrick tsked. "Well, it did seem you were implying something."

Hell help me.

Nolan pointed his finger at me. "But you—"

"Enough!" the oracle said, her voice echoing through the almost empty ballroom. Everyone fell silent. She continued in her regular tone, "That's enough. We should—"

"Wait," Dorian interrupted her. "You're the fucking oracle. How come you didn't see this? How come you didn't sense Reynard was in danger?"

She turned her hard gaze toward him. "I don't have to explain the logistics of my gift to you, worm." Dorian stepped forward, looking like he would barrel into her, but Alex's arm shot out in front of his chest, stopping him. "However, I'll say this. I don't choose when the visions come. They happen whenever they want and they can be about anything they want. It's not my call."

"What a great oracle," Nolan said in a low voice, even though we all could hear him quite clearly.

I could feel the tension radiating from all of them—from all of *us*. Soon, a fight would start.

I opened my mouth to try to put some order to this the mess, when Roberta, Reynard's main consort, stepped forward. Her eyes were rimmed with red and her lips trembled.

But, even through her pain, she lifted her head and stared at each one of us. "You were his princes, the men he trusted with his life, with his family. I don't care if you have problems with each other. For him, for Reynard, put it aside and work together to find who did this. Then avenge him."

I lowered my head in respect. "You're right, Lady Roberta. We'll start on it right away."

She nodded in response. Her gaze fell on the man on the floor who had spent the last three hundred and some years by her side. Tears filled her eyes. With a whimper, she turned around and hurried out of the ballroom. The other three consorts and two guards followed her.

"The mourning period starts now," Sarki said, her voice with the same authoritative timbre I had only seen her use a handful of times before. She met my eyes, raising one eyebrow at me, as if she wanted to pass me a secret message. "Peacefully, we'll arrange for Reynard's and the guards' proper burial, and we'll mourn them for ten days. After that, we'll find who did this and we'll make the traitor pay."

Everyone nodded in agreement. One by one, they left the ballroom, until only Alex and I were left—with the dead.

I knelt beside Reynard's body and laid my hand over the silver cross pendant resting on his chest. "I'll find whoever did this to you. I promise."

Alex snorted. "Don't pretend to be innocent. I know it was you. And I'll prove it."

He snarled, then marched out of the ballroom with the others.

Well, he was sure it was me, and I was sure it was him. I just had to find a way to prove it.

7

THEA

I GAPED AT THE PRINCE'S BACK AS HE DASHED DOWN THE HALL, faster than lightning. He was leaving Judy and me alone with this human boy?

"Come with me," the boy said, his voice still in that weird, shifting tone teenagers possessed. "I'll take you two to Prince Drake's chambers."

He started walking down the hallway, and having no other option, I followed. We crossed a long corridor, then turned into another sweeping staircase. The landing atop the stairs opened into a wide archway where two vampires stood guard, and into an empty room. The boy hurried to the double black doors on the other side of the room.

There, he paused, propped a knee up, on which he rested Judy's back, and fished out a big, black key from a necklace under his shirt. He put it into the lock, and like magic, several other invisible locks turned, one by one, their clicking sounds echoing in the empty room.

Finally, the clicking stopped, and the boy opened the door.

I followed him in and gawked at the place.

There was no black and burgundy here. In fact, it seemed we had entered a modern house by the ocean instead of a corner of a dark castle. I crossed a short foyer, then walked around the large sitting room, my boots ticking on the cream stone floors. I ran my fingers along the back of the beige leather sectional and scanned the many light brown book-cases spread around the room—all filled with books and scrolls.

Two steps led up to a dining room where a beautiful glass table and eight beige leather chairs took most of the space. I pulled out a chair and sat on it, inclining my head so I could admire the long, glass chandelier. A thin sheet hung by metal cords in the corners, and atop it, dozens of lit candles, all in tones of beige, soft yellow, light green, and light blue.

It was beautiful.

Almost as beautiful as the floor-to-ceiling window over-looking the gardens and the thousands of twinkling lamps illuminating it, almost like a mirror of the night sky. As if in a daze, I went to the window and rested my forehead on the cool glass. There was no moon tonight, but the many bright stars did a good job of being pretty by themselves.

"This way." The boy's voice snapped me awake.

"Right," I said.

Right. Judy. Me. Castle filled with vampires.

I followed the boy into yet another wide corridor, which had the same cream stone for floors and plain, beige walls. Double white doors were at the end of the long corridor, and I was guessing that was where the prince actually slept.

"In here." The boy opened a white door on the left. "You can stay here until Prince Drake returns." He walked into the bedroom and deposited Judy on the king-sized bed. He pressed a towel against her wounds, but the blood there had dried.

I stayed by the door, too afraid to go in. Too afraid to get close to the girl who was too pale to be alive. "Will she live?"

The boy lifted his hazel eyes to me. "I'm not sure." He pulled the light blue covers over her and then walked back to me. "I'm Thomas."

"Thea," I whispered.

"I don't know what is going on, but my master said to keep you in here until he got back. Please, don't cause any trouble for me and do what he asked." He gestured to the inside of the room. Reluctantly, I stepped inside. "Good. I am going to see if I can find any valerian salve for your friend. I'll be right back."

Thomas walked out of the room and closed the door. The lock clicked in place.

Panic rushed into my chest and my breathing grew shallow.

Shit, shit, shit.

Getting involved with Judy, standing up for her, and ending up kidnapped by a vampire was definitely not part of the plan.

I fell back on one of the four armchairs by the big window and rubbed my eyes with the palms.

Shit, shit, shit.

What was I supposed to do now?

A moan came from the bed and I froze. What *was* I supposed to do now?

Slowly, I approached the bed, but Judy was still sleeping. Or whatever she was doing. I placed two fingers on her wrist. It took me a moment, but I found her faint pulse.

A burning sensation prickled behind my eyes, and I

blinked, refusing to cry. I wouldn't cry. I wouldn't cry for Judy, I wouldn't cry for me, I wouldn't cry for this situation, I wouldn't cry for my plan getting screwed up.

I didn't know how long had passed, but I jumped two feet back when the lock turned and the door opened.

Thomas entered the room, a tray in his hands. "Hey. I thought you might be hungry." He placed the tray filled with food on the small, glass table among the armchairs, then picked up a vial from the tray. He approached the bed. "This is for your friend. It'll help with the pain."

"She's in pain?"

He leaned over Judy and poured a few drops of the golden liquid into her open mouth. Then he glanced at me. "I'm not sure. Usually, a vampire's bite is pleasant, but if the vampire wants, he can inject venom into his victim, causing pain later."

I tilted my head at him. "H-how are you here?"

He offered me a sad smile, which made him look older than he probably was. "You mean, alive and working for Prince Drake?" I nodded. "I had just turned eight when my invitation came. It was for my family and I. It was one of the happiest days of our lives. Until they locked the ballroom's doors and attacked us. I don't really know what happened. The elixir didn't work for me. I was dizzy, but I was conscious. I knew I was in a bad situation and had to leave." He clasped his hand in front of him. "Prince Dorian and Prince Albert came for me. They started fighting each other, saying my blood was sweet and they both wanted it. For some reason, Prince Drake stepped in and claimed me before they touched me."

He had been only eight years old, so it was before the minimum age was raised to fifteen.

"So ... he just claimed you? A vampire can do that?"

Thomas nodded. "It's one of their rules. If a prince wants to claim a human, he can. A prince can have as many humans as he wants and do whatever he wants with them. And the others can't touch the claimed human. Unfortunately, we're still called blood slaves, like the others."

"And that was ...?"

"Eight and a half years ago."

"How many times have you tried to escape?" Because he had to have tried, right?

"None." Drake's rough voice shook the windows as he came inside the room. I flinched and took two big steps back. The prince faced me, his green eyes hard. "Thomas knows his life depends on my generosity, so he follows my rules." Without averting his eyes from mine, he said, "Thomas, you may leave now."

"Yes, my prince." The boy bowed his head, and then scurried out of the room, closing the door behind him.

Drake walked to the other side of the bed. His gaze fell on Judy. "Her heartbeat is even weaker now."

"Isn't there anything you can do?"

"She has lost too much blood," he said, his voice low. "Not even a transfusion can save her now. Besides, I believe she has venom in her veins." He raised his head, and his gaze met mine again. But this time, his eyes weren't hard. They were ... sad? "The only way to save her is to turn her, but I'll argue that's not actually saving." He let out a long breath. "I can't turn her."

Couldn't or wouldn't? It didn't matter. If it were me in that bed, I wouldn't want anyone turning me. I had no idea what Judy wanted, but this wasn't part of the plan. My caring for a stranger wasn't part of the plan. She was supposed to have died in the ballroom or be taken with the others—for later.

"So ... I just watch her die?" My voice broke at the last word.

Drake picked up the vial with golden liquid from the nightstand. "This will take away her pain. Two drops every hour until she's gone."

He set the vial back down, and then went to the door. He twisted the knob.

He was leaving. He was leaving me here, locked like a helpless princess in a tower. What was I supposed to do? What happened next?

"What about me?" I hadn't intended to ask that aloud, but the words flew out of my throat.

Drake paused and glanced at me over his shoulder. "I ... some important things need my attention now. I'll be back soon and we'll talk."

I gulped. "Talk about what?"

"About what I expect from you."

8

DRAKE

AFTER NOT SLEEPING FOR FOURTEEN DAYS, I SLEPT TWO DAYS straight.

And I only woke up because Thomas, who apparently had a death wish trying to rouse a vampire from deep slumber, had told me that Reynard's celebratory dinner was tonight.

I groaned as I left my bed. That dinner ... that was something I didn't want to attend, but I had to. We would remember his life, honor his memory, drink and eat in his name, and I had to be there. For the man he had been, for the father he had represented, I had to be there.

So, I took a long bath, put on my nicest black suit, a dark red shirt, and black tie—DuMoir colors—pinned the brooch with the silver cross on my lapel, and walked out of my bedroom.

As usual, I found a tall glass and a wine-like bottle on the dining table. A small smile tugged at the corner of my lips. Thomas knew me well.

But instead of sitting down, I turned to him. "Please, bring Thea to me."

His eyes widened for a moment, but he bowed his head to me. "Yes, my prince."

Not a minute later, Thomas reappeared with Thea behind him.

She stared right at me, again full of false confidence. Other than that, she looked haunted, but well.

"Thomas, bring some food for Thea, please."

"Yes, my prince." Again, the boy bowed, and then left the room.

I gestured to the dining table. "Please, sit." Thea hesitated, but she finally took a chair in the middle of the table. I sat at the head, where my drink awaited me. "I see you found the clothes I asked Thomas to retrieve for you."

She looked down at blue and white summer dress, one of the simplest pieces of clothing Thomas had found in the castle for her. "Yes, thank you." Then, she froze and turned those bright gray eyes to me. "Please, don't tell me the clothes are from ... the dead."

I swallowed a chuckle. "No, those clothes were bought for the humans that are still in the castle. If you need, we can buy you more."

Her little nose scrunched. "Are there many humans in the castle?"

"You mean, blood slaves like Thomas and you?"

"Y-yes."

I paused, wondering why she was asking me that. Did it matter? I was certain that she couldn't escape, and if she tried ... well, that would be her bad. "Not many. Two dozen. Maybe a little more."

I poured some of the blood into my glass. Her eyes

widened, and then she averted her gaze, her hair falling like a curtain, hiding her face from me. For some reason, I didn't like that.

After a long moment of silence, she lifted her head and stared out the window at the setting sun. The orange streaming through the glass gave her fair skin a sun-kissed tone, and her gray eyes turned even brighter, almost transparent. Her full, red lips parted as she inhaled deeply. It was hard not to notice how her delicate features went well together. It was hard not to notice how pretty she was.

And her scent ... I inhaled deeply, savoring her sweet, sweet scent. It was pure temptation.

"What happened to Judy's body?" she asked in a whisper.

Judy had died not long after I had left their room two days ago. Thomas told me Thea had been in complete shock while he picked up the body and took it away.

"We aren't animals, you know. Well, for the most part." I sighed, not in the mood to explain what I meant by that. "There's a human graveyard a couple of miles behind the castle, at the edge of the forest. Thomas and Lewis buried her there."

Thea's eyes filled with tears, but she wiped at them before they could fall. Then she looked at me again. "Is that where I'll be buried when you kill me?"

"I saved you. Why would I kill you now?"

"You're a vampire. You're a monster. That's what you do."

I inhaled sharply. What kind of romance novels was this girl reading? Weren't authors portraying vampires like some kind of special heroes now?

"Thomas has been with me for over eight years, and I plan on making sure he has a long life."

"While imprisoned in this castle. Do you think that is life?"

"Better than to be used like a blood bag and be killed, don't you think?"

She pressed her lips together, her eyes fuming. "I'm not so sure."

This girl ... was she this stubborn? This prickly? If she kept that up, I wasn't sure how long I would endure her. "All right, here's the deal. You're mine now, which means no other vampire can touch you unless I agree to that. And I don't plan on doing that." Her heartbeat skipped a beat and then accelerated. "And I won't touch you either. You don't need to worry about that." I heard a slight relieved sigh coming from her lips. "You're free to walk inside my chambers for now. You can go anywhere but my bedroom. In a week, we'll reevaluate this. Meaning, if you prove to me that I can trust you, I'll let you wander in the castle. But, when and if that happens, I would advise you to ask Thomas to go out with you the first few times. It's easy to get lost." I paused for effect. "You know what happened at the feast. Things are crazy here right now, so I also advise you to steer clear of the other princes."

"You said they won't touch me without your consent."

"Right. And we wouldn't kill the man who opened his arms to us and tried to make us all into one big, happy family." She flinched. Hell, I shouldn't be scaring her so much. "Anyway, once you earn my trust, I'll let you go out from my quarters and in the castle. Then maybe, someday, even go outside."

Her eyes widened. "Outside?"

"Outside the castle, still within the estate limits."

A knot appeared between her brows. "I'll never be able to leave again, will I?"

Why was it so hard to answer her question? "No," I said, my tone harsher than I intended. "Do you understand the rules?"

Instead of answering, she asked, "What if I don't follow them?"

Hell. "I'll have to put you with the other humans."

Her throat bobbed. "The ones saved for later?"

I nodded. "Now you see I'm trying to help you?" She didn't answer. So I asked again, "Do you understand the rules? Will you follow them?"

A new, watery shine fell over her gray eyes. "Yes."

"Good." I pushed away from the table and stood. "Thomas will be in shortly with your food. Then, he'll escort you back to your bedroom."

Without looking at her again, I went to the door, used the black key to unlock it, and left my chambers. I leaned against the locked doors and finally breathed deeply—the moment she stepped foot out of her bedroom, her sweet scent had been everywhere. Even her friend's blood, with her open wound, hadn't called to me the way Thea's did.

I swallowed hard.

What the hell had I been thinking? Inviting this girl to live in my chambers? To be my charge? My blood slave? It was a ticking bomb living across the hall. The only way to contain myself, to contain the hunger, was to keep myself away from her.

I marched down to the biggest dining room in the castle, where six tables of forty armchairs fit comfortably. I took my place at the head of the second table, with Lewis and Holden, two of my men, by my sides. Alex was at the other end of the table, accompanied by Ralf and Eden, two of his men. Nolan, Cain, Gray, Phelps, and Albert were already in their places.

Patrick, Aston, and Dorian arrived soon after and took their seats. The only seat left empty was Reynard's at the head of the table, and it was covered by a black veil.

The oracle sat to the left side of the empty seat, Roberta was on the right, and beside her the other three consorts. The rest of the tables were filled by the other members of our house—all vampires who meant something to Reynard, who he had brought into his family.

Twenty vampire guards lined the walls and watched over the exits. And, from the report I had received right before entering the room, I knew there was about forty more patrolling the garden outside.

Hopefully, no tragedy would strike tonight.

When it seemed everyone was in the room, Sarki stood from her seat and faced us all. "A great misfortune fell over this house. We lost our leader, our guide, our friend, our mentor. Reynard might be gone, but his legacy will live on. Tonight, we'll drink and eat for him." As she said it, human slaves, wearing plain dark gray dresses and pants and shirts, came into the room, each one bringing a tray with bottles of blood and big goblets. "We'll tell stories, our stories and his stories. We'll remember him and honor him. We'll sing songs in his name." The humans deposited the bottles and goblets on the names, and then stood there, two steps away, in reach of any of us who preferred the fresh thing. One of the slaves poured blood into Sarki's goblet. Without acknowledging the human, she took the glass and raised it high. "For Reynard."

"For Reynard," we all toasted.

I lazily took my glass and sipped from it while most of the vampires reached for the humans for a quick bite. I averted my eyes and found Sarki watching me. She raised her goblet to me, as if toasting something else and only with me. Tired of these games, I nodded toward her, and then took a sip of my drink.

Her lips smeared with blood, Sarki let go of her goblet and stood. Her eyes roamed the room, filled with amusement, while she walked up to me. She leaned into my chair and whispered in my ear, "Have you already deciphered my vision?"

My brows slammed down. In all this confusion, I had forgotten about her vision. "No," I confessed, now thinking about her words.

It has arrived. It's here. It has come. The missing piece holding our salvation. Your salvation. Find the new and unite it with the old.

She ran her long, red nails along my shoulders. "Perhaps it's tied to the mystery surrounding us. Perhaps if you solve it, you'll find Reynard's killer."

Why would my salvation be connected to Reynard's death? He had been my salvation long ago.

Sarki turned her sugary smile to me, and then sauntered to the corner of the room, where three blood slaves stood with instruments.

"Play," she ordered, her tone absolute.

The humans started playing a classical tune—missing a few notes with their trembling hands—just like the ones Reynard liked so much.

Vampires stood from their seats. Some mingled, some danced, some drank from their blood slaves. Sarki danced in front of the improvised band, moving her curves in a sensual way.

My eyes followed her hand as it ran from her waist down her hips.

My throat grew dry, and I reached for my glass. After two

long gulps, I set my glass down and found Alex standing beside my chair. With his trademark snakelike grin, he shooed Lewis from his seat, then plopped down. He propped his elbows on the table, steepled his fingers, and turned his malicious grin to me.

"Where is your pretty blood slave? The blond one?"

Something like rage coursed through my veins and I gritted my teeth. "Safe."

"Safe ..." Alex repeated, finding my choice of words amusing, I was sure. "She's a pretty one. Beautiful, actually. You wouldn't be interested in sharing, would you?"

Under the table, my hands curled into tight fists. It was all I could do not to jump over the table and grab him by the throat. "Stay away from her," I warned, my tone low. Hard.

His grin widened. "Or what?"

He didn't want to know.

Before I could answer, Karl approached Alex and whispered something into the prince's ears. Alex's grin faded, and his jaw set into a hard knot. Unease grew in my stomach. What in hell could have wiped the damn smile from Alex's face?

Without looking at me, Alex pushed up and followed Karl to the other side of the dining room.

I let out a long breath and drank another big swallow of blood, trying to tell myself there was nothing wrong, that there was nothing going on. Besides the death of our beloved leader and not knowing who had committed such a crime, there was nothing wrong.

The ball of anxiety expanded and I shot to my feet.

To the hell with this party.

Careful about knowing eyes, I sneaked out of dining room and jogged back to my chambers. The guards weren't in their spot by the archway, but that wasn't uncommon, as they patrolled the entire level every few minutes.

But my breath caught when I slipped my key into the lock and the door swung open. I hurried inside, sure I would find Alex's men all over my place, trashing the rooms after having taken Thea to him.

The living room was intact, though.

"Thomas?" I called.

Without thinking, I turned into the hallway and marched toward Thea's bedroom. The door was open, and right under the threshold, broken glass shards littered the floor with Thomas lying unconscious amid it all.

My blood turned into ice.

Thea was gone.

9

THEA

DESPITE EVERYTHING THAT WAS GOING WRONG, I COULDN'T deny being in Prince Drake's chambers was better than being locked up somewhere underneath the castle with the other unclaimed humans. Here, at least, I had my own bedroom, my own bed, regular clothes, and real food ... the steak was buttery and on point, and the baked potato was covered in a sweet and sour sauce I had never dreamed of before—and it was oh so good.

However, I had no idea how I would continue my plans.

Thomas eyed my empty plate. "Done?" He had been standing along the wall like a perfect statue while I took my time eating. I tried engaging him in conversation once or twice, but he didn't say more than half a word to me, so I gave up. Besides, he was too young and probably innocent. He wouldn't know anything.

"Yes," I said, not ready to go back to the bedroom, where I was sure I would be locked in again.

Like a gentleman, he pulled out my chair and gestured for

me to walk toward the hallway. Like a lady, I stood and headed that way.

But instead of letting him escort me to my bedroom, I cocked my head at him. "Why haven't you tried to escape?"

Thomas didn't seem fazed by my question. He was young, but he was already taller than I was. And probably stronger too. "Because I owe Prince Drake. He is a good master. You'll learn that if you do as you're told."

I scrunched my nose, not liking the idea of having masters or doing as I was told. "It can't be just that."

"It is. Didn't you hear him? If I didn't stay here, I would have been moved down to the slave quarters, and believe me, you do not want that." He shuddered.

"I'm not talking about that; I'm talking about escaping."

"No one tries to escape and lives," he warned. "I mean it. Everyone who has tried was brought back to the castle and drained right away." He gestured once more to the hallway. "Now, please."

I sucked in a sharp breath and dragged my feet toward the hallway. With each step that echoed on the beige stone floors, the desperation inside me grew.

I couldn't be locked in the bedroom. I would go crazy, and it wouldn't help my cause. I had to do something.

I stepped into my bedroom and turned to Thomas, my eyes pleading. "Please, don't lock the door."

He looked down as if the weight of my gaze was too much for him. "I'm sorry."

Damn it. I didn't want to have to do this. "No, I'm sorry." I grabbed the vase from one of the small tables decorating my bedroom and slammed it into his head.

The boy fell to the floor.

My heart reared for a brief moment, hating what I had done, but there was no time to waste. I pulled the big black key from under his shirt and raced to the front door.

Praying the locks would be silent this time, I unlocked the door, opened it slightly, and spied out. To my surprise, the guards weren't standing by the archway on the other side of the room. I took that as a sign.

My heart hammering in my chest, I ran.

I had paid attention to the corridors and staircases we had taken to get here, but the castle was much bigger than I anticipated. When I had to turn away from the corridor we had first come through because a vampire guard was coming that way, I entered another long hallway lined by many doors and more archways leading to other corridors. I was instantly lost.

Damn it.

I stopped in the middle of a dark corridor and glanced from side to side. What now? Test the doors? What if I opened one and ended up face-to-face with a vampire?

I had to find a stairwell or some other way to go down.

Heavy footsteps echoed through the hallway and my heart stilled.

Eyes wide, I glanced at the many doors, doing a silent *eeny meeny miny moe* in my mind, trying to decide which one to use, until I saw a door that wasn't closed. Holding my breath, I pushed it open a little more and spied inside.

The dim light from the corridor illuminated long shelves with linen and buckets and brooms. A closet.

I slipped inside and closed the door, being careful with any sounds, then retreated to the back of the small room. I put my hands over my nose and mouth, trying to control my erratic breathing. With the vampires' enhanced hearing, it would be a miracle if they didn't find me in here.

The sound of the footsteps got closer and closer, and when they finally were upon the closet's door, I stopped breathing all together.

The footsteps slowed and my heart went into overdrive. I closed my eyes and prayed—it was all I could do right now. Holding my breath for too long, I was sure I was turning blue, until finally, the footsteps continued down the hall, in the same normal rhythm as before.

I was purple when I dared to breathe again.

Tears of relief and desperation filled my eyes. Holy crap, how would I make it through this castle like this? First, I was lost, and second, this place was crawling with vampires. They would hear me coming a mile away.

But I had to try. By all sacred things in life, I had to try.

I leaned on the door and listened, but no other footsteps or voices reached my ears. With trembling hands, I opened the door and spied out. I sneaked out of the closet and resumed my trek, my heart thundering faster inside my chest, my hands shaking harder, and my breathing uncontrollable.

I ran the opposite way the vampire had gone and stopped by the next archway connecting with another long hallway.

What now? Which way would I go? How could I keep running inside this damn castle and not expect to get caught?

It didn't matter. I had to try.

Taking a long, shuddering breath, I turned toward one of the corridors and marched on. I didn't stop at the next intersection. I didn't let myself. I had to keep moving, to keep going, to finding a way—

I bumped into a hard wall and bounced back, losing my balance.

A hand closed around my elbow before I could fall on the stone floor and kept me upright.

My breath caught.

Drake watched me with rage in his eyes.

10

THIS GIRL ...

Her eyes took up half of her pretty face, and her breathing came out in shallows gasps. "Y-you ..." she whispered.

Her heart beat as if she had run a marathon and her scent ... I let out a long breath before I either slapped some sense into her, pushed her against the wall and tasted her sweet, sweet blood, or threw her over shoulder and locked her in the dungeons.

Instead, I slipped my hand from her elbow to her wrist and held on tight. "What the hell were you thinking?" I asked, barely controlling my rage. "I told you not to try to escape."

Even though the fear was stamped in her gray eyes, she lifted her chin and faced me with a little defiance. "I'm not your pet."

"No, but you are mine nevertheless."

Mine ...

The idea of having her just for me both excited and terrified me. If only she behaved, I could pretend she didn't exist.

"You can't keep me here against my will."

Did she really think she could escape from a castle full of vampires?

"Watch me," I snarled. I tugged on her wrist. "Let's go." I marched down the hallway, dragging her behind me.

She whimpered, jerking against my hold, but I only increased the pressure. If it hurt, so be it. She deserved it.

Her scent filled my nostrils and I stiffened, clenching Thea's wrist tighter. She jerked against my hold again, but I only pulled her closer.

"Well, well, well," Alex said as he turned the corner and faced us. "What do we have here?"

I halted, keeping Thea behind me. "I thought you would be at the dinner," I said, willing my tone to remain casual, non-caring.

"I could say the same thing of you." His predatory gaze slid toward Thea. "But now I see why you left early. If she were mine, I would have done the same thing." He took one step closer. "Hello, pretty pet."

I tugged Thea even closer to me, gluing her to my back. Her hands fisted on my jacket. "Do not talk to her, Alex."

"Oh, but she's irresistible, brother. Beautiful and enchanting like a siren." He winked at me. "I meant it. After you're done with her, I wouldn't mind having my share of her."

I growled, a low rumble deep in my chest. "Stay away," I warned, putting all the menace I could muster into my gaze. He knew me. He knew I wasn't joking.

I put my arm over Thea's tense shoulders and steered her away from the evil prince. "Good night, Alex."

In silence, I guided a trembling Thea back to the chambers. Each step between us and Alex eased some of the tension coiled in my muscles.

Once inside my chambers, I let out a long breath and released her.

She took several large steps away from me and glanced around. "Where's Thomas?"

"What do you care? You almost killed him."

She rolled her eyes. "I didn't kill him." She chewed on her bottom lip, drawing my gaze like a magnet. I averted my eyes. "Is he okay?"

"I took him to the infirmary to get checked, but he should be okay." I didn't know why I answered her. She was my blood slave. She answered to me. I stalked toward her. She retreated two steps until her legs bumped on the couch, but she faced me with her fake bravado. I towered over her, fighting the urge to bare my fangs to scare her more. "Listen to me, as I won't repeat this. Do not try to escape. Do not leave my chambers without my permission. Do not do anything without asking first."

She swallowed hard and her neck bobbed. My breath caught. "So ... I can't eat without asking first? How about taking a shower? Or peeing?"

My hands balled into fists. I groaned, ready to pounce on her. This girl was driving me crazy. Ignoring her words and not retorting was a challenge, one I gladly accepted. "Didn't you just see Alex out there? He was all over you. I promise you, if he puts his claws on you, he won't be nice like I am." My stomach turned with the idea of Thea alone with Alex. "If you want to live another year, another month, or even another day, you will do as I tell you. Got it?" She stared at me, barely breathing. "Got it?" I barked, raising my voice.

She flinched.

Hell.

Still, she didn't give up. "I'm not afraid of him," she snapped. "I'm not afraid of you!"

I snarled and my fangs itched to come out. "You should be."

Her shoulders sagged as if she finally understood. "Then if I can't escape ..." Her eyes turned into two silver pools rivaling the moon outside these walls. Alex was right. She was as beautiful and enchanting as a siren. "If I can't escape, then let me go," she whispered, her voice breaking. "Please, let me go."

I took a step back. "That's not possible."

Tears filled her eyes. "In that case, I just want you to know that I won't behave, I won't follow orders, I won't act like this isn't all crazy, like this isn't all wrong. I'm not anyone's pet or blood slave!" she shouted.

My blood boiled and I exhaled through my nose.

I needed time away from this crazy girl before I did something stupid. "Go ahead. Try escaping again if you're that stupid!"

I marched out and slammed the damn doors. They rattled against their hinges. Since I didn't trust her, I locked the doors and turned toward the guards standing by the archway. "Stay here until I come back. That girl isn't supposed to leave."

"Yes, my prince," one of the guards answered while the other bowed his head in acknowledgment.

In need fresh air and space, I marched out of the castle and into the back garden. Breathing in an out and hoping all the anger and frustration left my muscles with each exhale, I walked around the maze.

I crossed paths with two guards patrolling the area, who bowed to me when I approached, then I marched until I was at the edge of one of the many artificial lakes on the estate.

The moon, only a thin sliver in the dark, reflected in the dark water, shimmering and trembling.

Hell, what had I done? By claiming that girl, I had damned my sanity, I was sure. She would drive me insane in no time. If I didn't lose my temper and drain her in the next ten hours, it would be a miracle. How was I supposed to keep her safe and protect her when even I couldn't endure her presence?

I wished I had never claimed her. I wished I could simply drop her at the blood slaves' quarters and forget her. But how could I? The moment I did that, Alex would take her. He would flaunt her around to spite me.

There had to be another way.

Please, let me go.

Her words twisted in my chest like a knife in my dead heart.

If only I could ...

But I could do nothing for her now. She was mine, and I had to take care of her, to make sure she was safe, even if she drove me crazy and made me want to squeeze her neck every two seconds.

I shook my head.

If anything, this at least made my long days, my long years, more eventful.

After another stroll around the maze, I headed back to the castle. As instructed, the guards were still in their spots.

"Anything to report?" I asked as I approached them.

"No, my prince," Tank said. "No one came in or out."

I nodded, then unlocked the door and stepped in.

I braced myself, ready for another round of argument, but

stopped dead in my tracks when I saw her lying on the couch, sleeping with her long blond hair fanned out over a pillow, and a book on her lap.

I picked up the book and stared at the cover. *Dracula* by Bram Stoker. I almost laughed at her reading choice. I turned to put the book back in its place on my shelves, but stopped. If she was reading it, then there was no reason to put it away. I dropped the book on the coffee table in front of the couch, then glanced at her.

The sofa was comfortable, but sleeping here wouldn't be good for her back. Careful not to wake her, I picked her up in my arms, alarmed by how small and fragile she was, and carried her to her bedroom. Her head lolled back before she turned her nose to my chest. Something warmed inside me, but I pushed it down. Away. Back.

I gently laid her on the bed, took off her shoes, and pulled the covers over her.

Then I stood there, watching her. Watching her fair skin and the freckles on her nose, the long lashes resting over her cheeks, the small nose, and the full, red lips. Her hair was pure gold around her, like the sun's halo.

She was beautiful and enchanting.

The urge to protect her, to keep her safe, hit me square in the chest, taking my breath away.

I didn't understand why I felt this way about her, why I wanted to make sure she was okay and would be okay. I didn't understand why I felt so drawn to her, but I couldn't ignore it anymore.

11

I DIDN'T REMEMBER MOVING FROM THE COUCH TO THE BED LAST night. It only could have been Drake, but I wasn't about to question it.

After taking a shower, I went to the closet and inspected the clothes in there. I recognized my own clothes—my jeans and blouse and my ballet flats—and the beautiful dress I had used during the ball, but the rest wasn't mine. Even after three days, I still didn't know everything in here.

There were blouses and tees and shirts and skirts and shorts and pants and dresses of all colors and styles. Same for the shoes. And they were all my size.

Trying to feel normal, I picked a pair of capri jeans, a dark pink blouse, and ballet flats.

My hands shook as I reached for the knob. After our argument the night before, I wasn't so eager to face Drake again.

I groaned.

He drove me crazy. Why the hell did he have to be so infuriating? So possessive? Why the hell had he claimed me? To annoy the hell out of me? To have someone to scare?

Tall and wide and strong, with those deep eyes and hard jaw and chin, he did scare me—a lot—but I wasn't going to let him know that. Well, I was sure he could hear and sense it with the rapid beating of my heart and my erratic breath, but it didn't matter. I wouldn't *show* it to him.

My stomach growled and I gave in. Holding my head high, I marched into the living and dining room.

And found it empty.

I didn't know why, but I had expected to see Drake there. I glanced at the window outside. I had no idea what time it was since my phone had been taken, and there were no clocks in this house, but it looked like the sun had almost set. It was probably eight or nine at night, the time I thought Drake had breakfast.

I shuddered, remembering him drinking a tall glass full of blood.

"You're up," Thomas said, coming into the room from the other side. "I'll bring you breakfast."

Before I could answer, he was gone.

I took my seat at the dining table and stared at the night sky while I waited. Not five minutes later, Thomas placed a tray in front of me.

"Thank you." I looked at him. "And ... I'm sorry."

He shrugged. "I don't care. Just don't bother me anymore. Or break things on my head." His tone was curt, sharp. He was hurt and it was because of me. "You can leave if you want. I don't care."

I swallowed hard, trying to think of something to say and coming up short. He was the only human I'd had contact with in three days. In a sense, it was as if he was my only potential friend here, and I had shattered any possibility for a friendship last night.

Before I could stop, the words were out of my mouth. "Where's Drake?"

"*Prince* Drake," Thomas corrected me. "Today is Lord Reynard's funeral, so Prince Drake won't be back for a few hours." He glanced at me, his expression deadpan. "Do you need anything else?"

I glanced down at the tray in front of me. There was enough food to feed four of me here. "No, thank you."

Thomas grunted before disappearing behind a door.

My stomach growled once more, and despite my mood having turned sour, I ate my breakfast.

When I was done, I stood and glanced around.

Now what?

I bit my lip as an idea came to mind. Thomas said Drake would be out for hours, and as far as I could see, Thomas didn't want to be near me, which meant he wouldn't be coming this way anytime soon. It was a foolish idea, but the only one I had ...

I started with the living room. I rummaged through the tables, the shelves, behind the books, under the couch ... there weren't many drawers or places to hide anything in here. Everything was open, and most of the tables had glass tops and no drawers.

Another idea hit me.

The walls. Maybe there were hidden doors or compartments in the walls behind the furniture. I checked behind chairs and tables and wall decorations, but again there weren't many. There were no paintings on the walls, no picture frames, nothing.

Sighing, I moved on to the dining room. That took me even less time to check as there was only the long table, the chairs, and a glass buffet table along a wall.

Apprehensive, I turned toward the hallway.

The first door revealed a library of sorts. Beige shelves lined the walls, filled from the bottom to the top with more books and scrolls, and a long, leather chaise occupied the center. What was it about this vampire and books? With his menacing height and deadly stare, I didn't take him for a reader.

No. He looked like an assassin. Or a bodyguard. Or the rebel guitarist of a rock band.

Or a monster.

I shuddered, pushing those thoughts away.

I had to focus. I was here for a purpose. The sooner I—

Pushing those thoughts out of my mind, I went back to the hallway and checked the next door. A guest bedroom much like mine. The next four doors were suites; again, very much like mine. Then there was a small closet with extra linens and towels—I couldn't imagine vampires having guests and hosting them like normal human families did.

I searched through my bedroom too, though like all rooms on this side of the castle, there weren't many good hiding places in here.

Then, I halted in front of the double doors at the end of the corridor.

I stared at them, wondering, thinking. I shouldn't go in there. Drake would kill me. But he wasn't here. Even Thomas wasn't here. If I were quick, he would never know.

Besides, Drake's chambers were the only logical place anything of value could be hidden.

My hands trembled as I twisted the knob. I fully expected it to be locked, but it wasn't. The knob turned and the door swung open.

I held my breath and stepped inside.

My brows jumped to my hairline as I took in the room in front of me. Off-white ceramic flooring, a couple of thick beige rugs, a king-sized bed with a fluffy off-white comforter and pillows along a wall, a long but low lit fireplace on the opposite wall, and floor-to-ceiling windows on the other side of the room. Thick, white curtains bunched at the corner, probably for the daytime, when Drake was sleeping and wanted darkness.

It was beautiful, elegant, modern. So unlike a vampire.

Slowly, I walked through the place, stunned by how cold, how precise, how male his suite was. Well, his entire quarters. There were two doors beside the bed, one leading to an open bathroom with a big white marble tub and standing shower for at least ten people to shower simultaneously, and the other led to the most simple but long walk-in closet I had ever seen. A long bar ran from one side to the other and many shirts and jackets and dress pants hung from it. On the floor, a couple of pairs of shoes. And that was it. No drawers, no folded clothes stacking high, no drawers.

Where did he keep his underwear?

Did he even wear any underwear?

An image of Drake in only his underwear popped in my mind. Heat spread through my cheeks, and once again, I pushed unwelcome thoughts from my mind.

Carefully, I lifted the edge of his bed covers. To my surprise, I found a long silver dagger under a pillow. The blade was polished and sharp, and the hilt had swirly engravings. It was beautiful. I stared at the dagger a moment longer, wondering why a goddamn vampire would sleep with a dagger under his pillow.

And why did it matter? Shaking my head, I pulled the covers back on.

Standing beside the bed, I whirled around, letting my eyes scan the place, but there was nothing. No one—

My gaze snagged on a faint line on the wall. Frowning, I approached it and ran my finger over it. The line went straight down to the floor. Following it up, the line turned parallel to the floor. I gasped, realizing this was a door.

I pushed it with all my might, but it didn't budge. I tried slipping my fingernails into the cracks so I could pull the door, but the crack lines were too narrow.

I stepped back and looked at it. How was I going to open it?

Then something caught my eye. In the bottom left corner where the wall met the floor, the line was a tiny bit thicker. I knelt beside it and examined the opening. It was small and somewhat oval, with pointed edges.

I stared at it for a moment while the wheels in my mind turned. It couldn't be the black key Drake and Thomas carried around. Another key? But where could it be?

The dagger!

The shape was of the dagger's blade.

Excitement filled my chest as I pulled the blade from the under Drake's pillow and slowly slid its blade into the small hole on the wall. The blade went all in, and when the hilt touched the wall, a faint click sounded.

My eyes wide, I pulled out the dagger, and the door popped open with a loud whistle. My heart skipped a beat. Slowly, I pushed the door all the way open and spied inside.

Unlike the other rooms in this side of the castle, this one was like a big attic. It was a large room with a low ceiling and cluttered with objects. I could barely walk among the stacked things—a rocking chair, boxes with old toys, a rickety shelf filled with old leather-bound books, a broken vanity with shiny jewelry and empty perfume flasks ... everything forgotten and covered in dust and cobwebs.

A stack of frames caught my attention and I approached it. Curious, I ran my hand over the dust gathering on top of the first painting, cleaning some of it. It was a family. A father, a mother, three young boys, and a little girl—no older than two—all of them close together and smiling.

The bright green eyes of the oldest boy stared back at me.

I gasped and—

"What are you doing in here?" his voice shook the room. My heart seized in fright and I dropped the painting. It teetered on top of the others, then flopped to the dusty floor. Drake was by my side in a second, picking up the painting. He turned his dark glare to me. "What are you doing here?"

"I ... I ..." I didn't know what to say. Should I lie? What would I say? There was no reasonable excuse for me to be in here. "I'm sorry," was all I could think to say.

He growled at me. "You shouldn't be in here. You shouldn't even come near my bedroom!"

I swallowed my fear and faced him. "I was bored."

He bared his teeth. "Bored? That's your excuse?"

"There's nothing to do here!"

"Then go read a book!"

"That's not enough. I need to go out!"

Drake punched the wall behind me, missing my head by an inch. I flinched. I could lie to him about not being afraid, but I knew he could hear my heart and breathing. He knew I was afraid of him.

"I'm tired of you. I'm tired of your arrogance and your childishness." His eyes darkened and his fangs elongated. "If you want to go out, then get out!" he bellowed, snapped his teeth only a couple of inches from my face. "Now!"

I blanched, my stomach dropped, and my hands shook.

That was it. I didn't care if he was protecting me as he said. I didn't care that I had a purpose, a reason to be here. I couldn't live among vampires and pretend everything was fine. I couldn't take this anymore.

My heart slammed in my ribs as I raced out of the bedroom, across the hallway, to the front door. Without slowing, I threw the door open and rushed out.

"Hey!" a guard called to me, but I didn't care. I just kept running.

In matters of seconds, I was lost, but I kept going. I needed to get away from Drake, to get away from his sharp teeth and his rage.

I turned a corner and almost ran into someone.

Prince Alex.

The blood drained from my face, and I stepped back as his lips spread into a wolfish smile.

"Aren't you Drake's pet?" he asked, teasing, like a cat playing with a mouse. "Where is your master?"

My hand slapped over my heart and my knees wobbled. I had left the brooch in Drake's chambers.

Shit.

Holding my breath, I took a step back. "H-he's ... I'm ... hm ..."

If the fear wasn't overwhelming all of my senses, I would have thought Alex was handsome, like the other princes. Tall, wide, with long, brown hair and hazel eyes, and a devilish grin. A grin that now wanted way more than I was willing to give.

He wetted his lips. "Speechless, I see. A fine asset in a beautiful woman." He prowled over to me, trapping me between a wall and him. The hair on the back of my neck and arm stood on end. "Are you lost, little lamb? I can help you." He ran a finger down my cheek. "I can take you to my chambers, and I'll show you what fun is."

I winced from his touch. "Never," I spat, sounding braver than I felt.

With a growl, Alex grabbed my chin and turned my face to him. "You'll learn pretty quickly." He bared his fangs and leaned into my neck.

Whimpering, I pushed him, but the man was made of steel. He placed an arm over my chest and pushed me harder into the wall.

"No," I croaked, slightly out of air.

"Just relax," he said, grazing his fangs on my neck. "You'll like it."

12

DRAKE

HELL.

This woman …

I exhaled through my nose, trying to regain some control. I almost snapped at her. I almost threw her against a wall and bit her, for hell's sake. What was wrong with me?

What was wrong with *her*?

I glanced around the storage behind my bedroom, accounting for all my things. My family's things. The little I had here was all I could save from their lives. Everything in here was over five hundred years old. Everything in here was my treasure, one I had never shared with anyone.

How did she find it? And why was she snooping around?

A new wave of rage rolled over my muscles, but I released another long breath. This wasn't the time to be angry with her. I had scared her, really scared her, and she had fled my chambers in a rush.

I should go after her before she found trouble.

After placing the painting of my family on top of all the

others, I turned and sped from my room, following her sweet, sweet scent to find her.

I navigated through the corridors, and as her scent become stronger, his scent hit me too.

I faltered, then sped some more.

"Get off her!" I boomed as Alex leaned down, ready to sink his teeth into Thea's neck. Welcoming the rage back, I pushed him off to the side. Alex grasped Thea's arm and pulled her with him.

A laugh rolled out of Alex's mouth as he turned Thea in his arms, pressing her back to his chest. He stared at me, a challenging glint in his eyes. "Lost your blood slave? Finders keepers." He leaned down and licked her neck. Thea whimpered. Her heart beat too damn fast.

"Let her go," I said with a low growl.

"But she smells so good," Alex said. "I don't remember her smelling this good when you first claimed her." He sniffed her neck and she flinched. "I bet her blood will be like heaven."

"Let. Her. Go," I repeated, fighting so I wouldn't lose my patience right here and murder Alex.

Alex made a show of splaying his fingers on Thea's stomach, grinding her against him, then showing me his fangs.

I lost it.

Fangs bared, I lunged at him. With careful movements, I pried Alex's hands from around Thea, grabbed her arm and spun her to stand behind me, and went for Alex's throat. Pressing him against the wall, I lifted him up and pressed my fingers tight, choking him.

He simply laughed. "Is that supposed to hurt?"

I pressed some more and his neck cracked. "How about now?"

His eyes went wide. A little more and I would break his neck. That wouldn't kill him, but he would be out for a while.

"What's going on here?" Dorian's voice was like a bucket of cold water over my head.

I let go of Alex and stepped back, purposely putting myself in front of a shaking Thea.

"My dear brother Drake was offering me his blood slave," Alex said with a wide smile. "Such a nice offer from him."

A growl rumbled in my chest.

Dorian wasn't fooled, though. He knew how much of an ass Alex could be, and he knew I wouldn't offer a blood slave to anyone.

Dorian turned to me. "Drake? Anything to add?"

"Alex is to stay away from my blood slaves," I snapped, making sure he heard the bite in my tone.

"But she just threw herself in my arms," Alex quipped. "There wasn't much I could do."

Fury swept through me and I advanced toward him.

Dorian raised a hand. "If you two insist on fighting, then make it a duel. We all know it was bound to happen one of these centuries. But out of respect, wait until the mourning period is over."

Alex turned his vicious smile at me. "What do you say, brother? Want to duel?"

I wanted to crush his head between my hands right here, right now. I pressed my mouth tight, making my jaw hurt. "Just ... stay away from my blood slave," I repeated.

Alex tsked. "I would prefer a duel."

"It is set, then," Dorian announced as if he would simply write duel on a long to-do list. "You two will duel after the mourning period."

I grunted in response, not trusting myself to say anything non-threatening if I opened my mouth.

Without taking my eyes from the devil in front of me, I reached for Thea behind my back. I found her shaking hands and tugged her closer. Then, I spun around, taking her under my arm and hurrying her away.

I practically carried her all the way back to my chambers, and once we were behind locked doors, I let go of her. She plopped down on the couch. I paced in front of her, trying to calm down before I growled at her and spewed more threats I didn't mean.

This woman …

She would be death of me.

"What …?" she whispered. I halted and turned to her, surprised to find she was staring at me with big, vulnerable eyes. Her hands, folded over her legs, still shook and her heart still beat too fast. "What does the duel mean?"

"It means Alex is challenging me for you."

Her face paled even more. "But … why?"

"Alex likes irking me. He knows stealing you from me will definitely irk me."

Her delicate brows turned down, as if the explanation didn't make sense. Besides irritating me, Alex knew Thea was pretty. Beautiful even. He had smelled her blood. He had been close to her—my insides burned at the image of her pressed against him. Alex knew I wouldn't drink her blood and abuse her, and that was exactly what he planned to do to her.

A new rush of anger coiled around my muscles, and I clenched and unclenched my hands.

She looked down at her lap. "I'm sorry."

Empathy invaded my chest, and I couldn't stop myself. I

knelt in front of her. "That was why I told you to stay inside my chambers. That was what I was trying to protect you from." She lifted her gaze to me, locking her pretty eyes on mine, as if searching for the answer to a burning question in them. "He isn't the only one that would use you to get to me. There are other dangerous and reckless vampires in this castle. They would see you out alone, and they wouldn't care about my claim on you. They would take you for themselves." Her shoulders curled and she became smaller and more fragile right in front of me. "You understand now?"

"Yes," she said, her voice weak.

An invisible hand closed around my dead heart and squeezed. "Are you hurt? Did he hurt you?"

She shook her head. "No, no. I'm fine. Shocked, but fine. I think."

"That's good." I ran a hand through my hair. "I'm sorry too. I didn't mean to frighten you. It's just ... I never go inside that storage room. The things in there, they are a part of me I don't like to remember. Old memories bring back too much pain."

"I'm sorry," she said again.

"It's okay. Just promise me you won't snoop around anymore, and that you won't leave my chambers alone again." She stared at me as if I was asking her to hand me one part of her soul. "Thea, you have to promise."

She let out a shaky breath. "I promise."

I sat in an armchair and sighed. Maybe if I gave her some random information, she wouldn't want to snoop around so much. Was that worth it, though? Why did she have to know more about me? But for some reason, I wanted her to know more about me. I had scared her and now I needed to gain her trust again.

"What do you want to know?" I asked.

Surprise flashed in her eyes. "Hm, I don't know. How about ... how old are you?"

One corner of my lips tugged up. "I was twenty-five when I was turned, and I've been a vampire for a little over five hundred years."

Her jaw popped open, but she closed it. "Was it Lord Reynard who turned you?"

A pang ran through my chest at the mention of my father's name. "Yes, and I've been with him ever since."

"When did you become a prince?"

That was a strange question. She was new here. Unless she had thoroughly questioned Thomas and he had answered her, which I doubted, she couldn't know much about how things worked here. "What do you know about being a prince?"

"Nothing," she said. "I just ... I'm basing my discoveries on folklore here, but aren't vampires sterile? So you and the other princes aren't really Lord Reynard's sons."

"Well, not all vampires are sterile. It's rare, but male vampires can have children with human females." Sarki was an example of that, though she didn't know who her parents were. All we knew was that Reynard had found her and brought her to our household. "But you're right. The other princes and I aren't Lord Reynard's sons. We were chosen after proving our worth in his army and in this castle. And to answer your question, I became a prince a few years after being turned." I paused. "Any more questions?"

She bit her lower lip. Something primal, something hungry twisted in my stomach, and I had to avert my gaze. "Tell me more about vampires. What can you do? Super strength? Super healing? Turn to dust with the sun? Garlic repels you?"

Of course, she would ask those things. "We have superior strength, healing, speed, hearing, and scent among other things. Garlic and holy objects don't do anything to us." I gestured to the brooch pinned to the lapel of my shirt. "When Reynard was a young vampire, there was a group of priests hunting vampires, and they used crosses to scare vampires away. It didn't work, of course, so when Reynard became powerful and created his own coven, he adopted this symbol as a joke."

"It's not that funny," she mumbled, as if she were offended by it.

I suppressed a grin. "What else? We don't need to eat anything other than blood, though sometimes we do because we miss some things, some tastes. We don't exactly turn to dust in the sun, but it burns our skins, and if we're exposed to it for too long, yes, it can kill us. We need sleep, but not as much as humans do. We have hearts, but they do not beat anymore, and we don't need to breathe, but we do it out of habit."

"How about compulsion?"

"Yes, we have compulsion."

"Does it work on other vampires?"

"Yes, if you are stronger than them."

"And how do you kill a vampire?"

From her tone, I knew her question was innocent, curiosity, but I couldn't help grin at her. "Trying to plot how to kill me and escape the castle?"

Her face blanched again. "No, no, I would never—"

"I know, don't worry," I assured her. "Killing us isn't easy because of all our abilities, but a stake to the heart or cutting off our heads usually does the trick. Best if you do both."

She swallowed hard. "That sounds gruesome."

"When you live for five hundred years and are in charge of a brutal army, gruesome gets a new definition." I watched her for a minute. Though she was still shaken, she looked better, calmer. "Are you okay now?"

"I ... I don't know." She frowned. "There's still too much to process, too much to accept." She glanced around the living room. "And I have to get used to the idea that I'll never leave this place again."

The sadness in her voice ...

I let out a long breath. "We can make a deal."

Thea sat up straighter in anticipation. "Like what?"

I almost smiled at her. "I'll let you walk around certain parts of the castle and the back garden, but you have to do it during the times I allow you to, and you have to take Thomas with you." I could make sure Alex and the other malicious vampires in the castle were busy before telling her she was free to go out. As for Thomas, he wouldn't like the idea, but he was an expert on avoiding the other vampires when needed. "Is that okay? Do we have a deal?"

Her eyes sparked with hope and her lips turned up in a faint smile. I felt a punch in my stomach and the air fled my lungs. She was too beautiful, and when she was somewhat happy? She was stunning.

"We have a deal."

13

I LOOKED UP FROM THE FOOD SPLAYED IN FRONT OF ME TO THE man seated at the table's end.

Vampires were monsters. Abominations of nature. But no one could deny how dazzling they looked. Drake had left it out of his tale last night, but I knew beauty was one of their superpowers. They lured their victims with their beauty. It was harder to escape them that way.

Like how my eyes kept going back to Prince Drake whenever he was in the room. I bet he had been handsome as a human, but as a vampire? He was breathtaking. It was hard to ignore how the white shirt hugged his strong shoulders and chest, outlining enough of the many muscles underneath, how his pants fit around all the right places.

Heat blossomed low in my stomach, and I focused on the fact that he was a vampire. A monster. He wasn't worth drooling over.

A monster ...

A monster who had claimed me and yet treated me with respect. A monster who protected me from other monsters. A monster who sat through breakfast with me and kept me company, even though he didn't eat.

A monster who had instilled real fear in me the night before. Every time I closed my eyes, two images rushed into my mind: Drake baring his fangs and yelling at me, and then the relief pouring over his muscles when we were safely back inside his quarters.

At first, I thought he would kill me, then he seemed appeased I was safe.

The vampire prince was like a walking contradiction.

"Is everything okay?" Drake asked me, his voice rough and deep.

I suppressed a shiver and offered him a small smile. "Yes, thank you." I cut a piece of bacon and shoved it in my mouth.

When I was done, Thomas appeared by my side. "Excuse me," he said, his tone tight. Then, he started cleaning up.

"I can do that," I said. After all, Thomas was a blood slave like me. I didn't like the idea of Thomas acting like my servant.

"It's okay," Drake said. "Thomas doesn't mind."

A vein popped in Thomas's neck, and I was sure he did mind.

After he took the plates away, I stood. Drake stood too—tall and powerful. I almost stepped back.

"So ..." I started, a little tense. "Am I allowed to go out today?"

"Yes." Drake nodded. "Thomas will return soon, and he'll show you around the castle."

It was all I wanted. However, I had no idea what I was going to do with Thomas.

"Thank you," I said, feeling lighter than I had in days.

"My pleasure." Drake bowed his head, his black hair

falling over his eyes, then he spun on his heel and left through the front door.

Curiosity welled in me, and I wondered where he was going. Which was silly. As a prince of such a big vampire coven, I was sure he had many responsibilities and duties to attend to.

Thomas returned from the door on the other side of the living room. I hadn't been through there yet, but I could only assume it was some kind of kitchen, or a buffet area with access to the real castle kitchen.

He leveled his unamused eyes at me. "Ready?"

I felt bad for the coldness he threw my way, since it was my fault. "Yes," I said, trying to sound chipper. Maybe if I were happy, it would rub off on him.

But I wasn't happy, not really. While I stayed inside this castle, I wouldn't be happy. I was afraid. I was weary. I was determined.

I was on a mission.

Thomas guided me across two sets of hallways, down a wide staircase—there it was!—to a large archway that opened to a long room.

"The art gallery," he announced as we walked by many paintings, statues, and art pieces, all of them with special placement and lights.

I didn't know much about art, but everything looked expensive. "Are they real?"

Thomas cocked an eyebrow. "What do you mean?"

"Like, if I see the Mona Lisa in here, should I assume it's a copy, or will it be the real thing?" Everyone knew about the rumors that the Mona Lisa at the Louvre wasn't the original one.

"They are the real thing," he said, his tone clipped.

After five long rooms filled with art, Thomas guided me to another part of the castle. Like before, an archway opened to a large room, but this time, there was more than paintings here.

"What is this place?" I asked, looking around with wide eyes.

"The museum."

Of course. A museum inside the vampires' castle, because why not?

Unbelievable.

But perfect. If I had to bet, the answer to my quest was right here.

I scanned the place with curious eyes. Like the art gallery, each item in here had a special place, a special encasement, a special spot, and special lights. But instead of paintings and busts and art pieces, there was ancient furniture, pieces of gold and silver, jewelry, huge boxes, small boxes, vials and jars of all sizes and shapes and colors, broken pieces of stones, headpieces, weapons, armor ... and so much more.

Now that I was here, this was the place I had been searching for. I was sure of it.

But I couldn't do anything with Thomas by my side. Though, as we walked around, I observed more than the exposed pieces. I took note of where they were placed, on top of pedestals or hung from the ceiling, if they were secured to their spots by nails, hooks, or glue, or simply deposited there, if there seemed to be any hidden compartments under them.

It was too much to see, too much to observe, but my mind and heart raced.

How in the world would I get rid of Thomas to explore this place for real?

The opportunity presented itself when Thomas took me

to the back garden and introduced me to the maze. A huge thing with hedges over eight feet tall that extended for miles.

"This is incredible," I whispered, gawking at it.

Thomas shuddered. "It's a nightmare."

"Have you gone through?"

"Through? No. I tried a few times and only got lost."

"How did you get out of there?"

"Prince Drake noticed I was missing and came after me."

I stared at him. "How long did you stay in there?"

His cheek reddened. "The longest? Almost six hours."

"Holy shit," I whispered, staring at the maze's entrance.

Six hours without Thomas and without Drake coming after me. I knew it was risky with the other vampires in the castle, but I couldn't do much to avoid that. I could only pray I wouldn't run into anyone.

"Come on." Thomas jerked his chin to the other side of the garden where lampposts illuminated a large fountain and stones benches.

"No, I want to go into the maze," I said, aware that I sounded like a five-year-old who wanted a lollipop before dinner. I stepped through the entrance and turned to him. "Come on. It'll be fun."

Thomas's skin blanched. "I don't want to spend another half day in there."

"Don't worry. I'm good with directions," I assured him. "I'll have us out the other side in no time. I promise." I hated lying, but it seemed like the only thing I could do in this castle.

I disappeared around the hedge.

"Hey!" Thomas called. "Come back." He huffed and puffed. Then he groaned. "Wait for me."

Three seconds later, he was beside me and we started our march through the maze.

Though I pointed where to turn, I kept half a step behind Thomas, and when I was sure he wasn't paying attention to me, I snapped a little branch off the hedge, right at waist level.

I waited twenty minutes, wandering around the maze as if I was sure how to get us to the other side, when in fact, I went around in circles, aiming for the middle of the maze, trying to make Thomas lost instead.

Then, I fell a step back. Then another. Then another.

Finally, Thomas took a turn several steps before me, and I ran off.

I heard him shouting my name as I sprinted back, following the broken branches until I was out of the maze. I paused at the maze's entrance and stared at the castle.

I would find it. Wherever it was hiding in there, be it in the museum or Lord Reynard's quarters, I would find it.

I took a deep, determined breath and made my way back to the museum, always careful to avoid the vampires.

Once I stepped back into the museum, eagerness rushed through my veins. God, it had to here. It had to.

Without wasting time, I started my search. Like I had done in Drake's quarters, I went item by item, pedestal by pedestal, spot by spot, and looked over everything. I searched the sides of the pedestals, underneath the items, inside boxes ... I even looked on the wall, searching for hidden doors like the one in Drake's bedroom.

The click of heels on the floor echoed through the large room. My heart thundering, I straightened and pretended to be admiring an old urn with hieroglyphs.

A woman with long brown locks and smooth dark skin

approached me. She had on a provocative red dress that hugged the generous curves in her body. She was gorgeous, and more importantly, she was powerful.

Smiling, she tilted her head. "Thea, isn't it?"

I swallowed hard. "Yes."

"I'm Sarki."

"The oracle," I said, knowing exactly who she was.

"That's right." Her smile widened. "I see Prince Drake told you about me." Not really. "He's a good master, isn't he?"

I shrugged, not sure what the purpose of that question was. "He's ... okay."

"And where's Thomas?" She glanced from side to side, looking for the boy.

"He had to run a quick errand," I lied. "He'll be back any minute."

"Of course," she said, and I was sure she didn't believe me. Her smile faded and her eyes gained a hard glint. "I heard Alex challenged Drake to a duel for you." She tsked. "With everything going on, Drake doesn't need that."

My hands trembled, but I lifted my chin. I hadn't cowered when Drake had threatened me; I wouldn't cower for a jealous woman who was trying to intimidate me. Even if she was a powerful oracle. "I didn't ask him to. He did all of that on his own."

"Because Drake has a good heart. He can't help gathering *pets*." She spat the word as if she had said worms instead. "And now all he has worked so hard to achieve will crumble if he loses a hell damned duel."

All he had worked so hard for? Like what? His position as a prince? What the hell was she talking about?

"There's nothing I can do—"

Suddenly, her eyes turned all white, and she said, "What

you look for is right in front of you. All you have to do is look." My heart stopped. Sarki blinked and her eyes returned to normal. She raised an eyebrow at me. "What was that about?"

"I ... I don't know." Right in front of me? Right in front of me were Sarki and the old urn, and I had already checked the damn urn and its pedestal.

"Are you sure? I can help you decipher the fortune," she said, her voice dripping with honey. "That's one of the things I did for Lord Reynard. I had the visions, and then I helped him decipher them."

"I-I really don't know what that meant," I lied, hoping her powers didn't involve detecting lies.

"All right." She stared at me with cloudy eyes. She didn't seem convinced. "If you think of something, let me know. I can help you."

She smiled, then sashayed out of the museum. I followed her with my eyes, and when she was gone, I let out a long breath, trying to calm my racing heart.

Could Sarki have it? But why? And where was she hiding it? It didn't make sense.

Heavy footsteps sounded from the other side of the museum. Deep voices reached my ears, though I couldn't make out what they were saying. But I was sure it wasn't Thomas or Drake.

My insides stilled.

All right, I was done for the day.

As fast as I could without drawing attention or bumping into anyone, I went back to the maze. I followed the broken branches until the last spot I had seen Thomas.

"Thomas!" I yelled. I went in farther, breaking the hedge branches like I had done before. "Thomas, where are you?"

"Thea!" I heard his voice, low and far. "I'm here!"

"Keep talking," I shouted back. "I'll find you."

"Talk about what?"

"I don't know." I advanced through the maze in the direction of his voice. "Tell me something about you."

"Like what?"

"What's your favorite color?"

"Green."

"Favorite food?"

"Five cheese lasagna."

"Hm, that sounds delicious."

"I can have the cook make one for you tomorrow, if you want."

I turned a corner and smiled at him. "I would like that."

Thomas rushed into me and wrapped his arms around my shoulders. "God, where were you?"

I disentangled myself from him, suddenly self-conscious that I had tricked him and he was now so happy to see me. Something like guilt snaked around my chest. "I guess I got lost. Sorry."

"It's okay, I guess." He glanced around the tall hedges and sighed. "We still have to find a way out of here."

"I might not know how to get to the end, but I'm pretty sure I can retrace our steps and find the entrance."

His eyes widened. "You are?"

I smiled at him. "Yup. Let's go."

As usual, Thea sprawled on the couch, her legs folded over the cushions, and her nose buried into a book. Today, she was reading the *Picture of Dorian Gray*.

Why didn't that surprise me?

However, what did surprise me was how much I liked watching her. Like she was at home, carefree and happy.

I knew she wasn't happy, though. I guess she would never be while she lived here—which would be until the day she died. Unfortunately, I couldn't let her go.

To be honest, even if I could, I wasn't sure I wanted to anymore.

As much as I fought it, I was getting used to her presence in my chambers. It had been nine days of constant watching —watching her having breakfast, watching her sweetly teasing Thomas when he was embarrassed over something, watching as she walked around the library and took her time choosing the next book she would read, watching as she ate dinner and bid me good night. She didn't know, but I sometimes watched as she strolled through the back gardens with Thomas.

Even her scent, as alluring as it was, had become a permanent fixture, something I craved, something I needed.

I frowned, thinking of the duel for her. The mourning period was almost over, and the duel was imminent. I couldn't lose to Alex. I couldn't.

"Something wrong?"

I smoothed my brows and willed my features into a neutral expression. "Nothing is wrong." Besides the duel and the fact that she was wearing a summer dress and half her thighs were exposed, her smooth, shiny skin a beacon to my senses, there was nothing wrong. "I just ... have something to do." She lowered her legs and sat up straighter. Her luminous hair fell around her shoulders, emphasizing her long neck and slender shoulders. I cleared my throat. "Do you need anything before I leave?"

She shook her head. "No. Thank you."

I bowed my head then zipped out of the room, too fast for her to follow.

Once outside, I took a deep breath. What the hell was I doing? Why did I care if she needed anything? Why couldn't I stop watching her? My mind wanted to explore a crazy answer I couldn't acknowledge, so I shoved those thoughts out of my head.

Tank, one of my guards, glanced at me. "Everything all right, my prince?"

I straightened my back. "Of course."

Without another word, I walked away. Going down the stairs, I passed a couple of blood slaves who bowed and didn't move until I was out of sight. They were probably going to some prince's chambers as a meal.

A growl rose from my chest as an image of Thomas or Thea becoming a simple food source flitted through my mind.

Once more, I pushed unwanted thoughts from my mind.

By the time I walked out of the castle and onto the largest stone balcony that opened up to the back garden, I had cleared my head.

I sensed her presence half a second before she appeared in front of me, and I barely stopped in my tracks before bumping into her.

"Hello, young Drake," Sarki said, grinning at me.

"Sarki." I dipped my head at her.

She glanced from side-to-side, her long, dark curls bouncing around her shoulders. Tonight, she wore a dark red suit and high heels that put her almost at my eye level. She returned her gaze to me, now serious. "Ready for the meeting tomorrow?"

"If it were up to me, we would have had this meeting days ago."

She tilted her head. "I heard about the duel. It seems we'll have to talk about that too."

I grunted. "Alex and his childish acts. Yes, we need to plan the duel."

She leaned closer. "Don't worry. I'll try to postpone it. Who knows? Hopefully, you'll be appointed as the new Lord DuMoir and then you can cancel the duel."

Now that made me anxious. As much as I would rather be lord of the castle over Alex, I wasn't sure I was ready to take on so much responsibility. Accepting becoming a prince and joining Lord Reynard's ranks had been a step I took so my existence wouldn't be lonely. I didn't mind obeying his orders and commanding his army.

But taking care of everyone in the castle? Vampires *and* humans? I wasn't sure I was ready for that.

"We'll see about that," was all I said about the matter.

Sarki reached out and placed a hand over my shoulder. "Don't worry. Whatever happens, I'll be by your side." Her voice was throaty, and her heart hammered inside her chest.

What the hell?

I took a step back and her hand dropped. "Thank you." I started walking past her.

Until she said, "I know what today is." I halted. "I know what you do on this night every year. Do you want company?"

I frowned. I guess after living in this castle for almost four hundred years, someone was bound to notice.

"It's okay." I glanced at her over my shoulder. "I prefer being alone tonight."

She offered me a small smile. "Well, you know where to find me if you change your mind."

"Thank you."

I turned and resumed my walk.

In no time, I stood atop a small hill at the end of the large garden. From here, I could see the lake and, on the other side, the village. During two days of the year, the village became a beautiful place with a luminous fountain, fancy restaurants, wine shops, antique stores, and happy people walking around. During the other 363 days, it was a simple place where low-ranked vampires lived with their blood slaves.

But no matter what, it still reminded me of home.

Before becoming a vampire, I lived in Europe with my family in a village much like the one across the lake. A village that was burned to the ground hundreds of years ago tonight.

I sat on the cold grass and watched the village's twinkling lights under the night sky.

15

THEA

Tired of being inside Drake's chambers, I asked Thomas to go with me for a stroll in the gardens. He didn't like it, but after a few emphatic pleases, he relented.

It was hard to say, but it seemed he was warming up to me. At least, I didn't get his glares more than twice a day now. While we took our usual walk around the maze—he never went inside with me again—I tried making him open up to me a little more.

"So, tell me," I started, forcing my voice to be innocent. Sweet. Friendly. "How is it to grow up in a castle full of vampires?"

He raised an eyebrow at me. "You mean as a blood slave?"

I cringed. "I mean ... yes, I guess that's what I mean."

He shrugged. "It's not like I have a choice, is it?" He stayed quiet for a moment. "I guess it could be worse. I was fortunate to be chosen by Prince Drake. Otherwise, I'm not sure I would be still alive." He lowered his voice as he said, "Most blood slaves don't last a year here."

My heart squeezed. "That is ..." I had no words.

"It's cruel," Thomas said it for me. "It's a terrible fate." He lifted his chin high. "Like I said, I'm grateful for Prince Drake. I'm sure I'll live a long life because of him."

But was it worth it? I tried wrapping my mind around living as a blood slave, even a well-treated one, and I couldn't. No privacy, no dreams, no friends, family. No freedom.

Well, it was not as if I had a choice right now either.

"What about friends?" I asked, trying to keep the subject less dark. "Were you able to make friends with any of the other blood slaves?"

"Here and there," he confessed. His cheeks gained a red tint.

"What is it?" I elbowed him in the ribs. "Tell me."

"There was this girl," he started, his voice low. "She was pretty and around my age. I liked her and I think she liked me, too." My chest constricted. I already knew how this tale was going to end. "Prince Nolan claimed her. She didn't last six months in his hands."

I rested my hand on his arm. "I'm so sorry."

He shrugged, making me drop my hand. "It's okay. It was a lesson. To not let my guard down or get attached to anyone here. It's not worth the heartache."

I wanted to tell him I was sorry again, but I couldn't muster the courage. At first, I hadn't given him much credit, but now I saw how strong and loyal Thomas was.

Maybe ... maybe if he showed me any signs that he wanted to escape, that he wanted a real life, I could include him in my plans. It would be harder, but if he wanted, I could try. We could try.

We strolled in silence a little while longer, while my mind wandered through different scenarios of how I would find out if Thomas would want to join me or not.

I was lost in thought when I spotted an unusual sight in the distance.

"What's he doing?"

Thomas followed my line of sight. "Oh yeah." He halted and stared at Prince Drake, who was seated alone atop a hill. From here, we couldn't see him well, but it seemed Drake was gazing at the lake. "He comes here on this night every year and sits there alone."

"Why?"

The boy pressed his lips tight before finally answering my question. "It's a special night for him." I took a step toward Drake, but Thomas grabbed my arm. "No. He prefers to be alone."

I stared at Drake, and for the life of me, I couldn't figure out why someone would want to be alone.

"Let's just check if he's okay." I jerked my arm free from Thomas's grip and approached Drake. I didn't know why, but from his reserved mien and tense body stance, this special night looked more like a sad night, and for some reason, I wanted to make sure the prince was okay.

I was still fifty yards from him when Drake said, "I thought Thomas said to leave me alone."

I halted in my tracks. Of course, he had heard my conversation with Thomas. He was a vampire. "He did, but I ignored him," I said, my tone normal since he would hear me anyway. Perfectly still, I waited three heartbeats. When he didn't protest again, I resumed my walk. I stopped again only a few feet from him. "Are you okay?"

His gaze wasn't on the lake. It was on the village. And I had been right. He did seem sad.

After a long moment, I didn't think he would answer me, and I was about to turn and leave, when he finally let out a long breath and said, "Tonight is the anniversary of my family's death."

"I'm sorry," I whispered.

"My family and I lived in a village like that one." He jerked his chin toward the other side of the lake. "I can't really explain why, but I come here every year and watch the village at night, as if my family was somewhere in there, asleep and dreaming of a better future."

Cautious, I took a large step toward him and lowered myself on my knees. "You miss them; that's why." Missing his family. Such a human feeling. Once more, Drake surprised me. He really wasn't like the other vampires. Curiosity welled inside me. He was a five-hundred-year-old vampire. His family had died a long time ago, but I wanted to know how. What happened to them? The courage to pose that question was missing. And before I could gather any, Drake turned his head and locked his gaze on mine, robbing the air from my lungs. The moonlight illuminated his pale skin and emphasized the sharp angles of his handsome face. By all that was sacred, I couldn't deny he was handsome. Heat crept up my cheeks. "I'm sorry." I started getting up. "I didn't mean to interrupt you."

"Stay." It had been low, almost a whisper, but I had heard it nevertheless. "I never wanted company before, but now that you're here, I don't feel like being by myself."

I should have gotten up and left. I should have scoffed in his face, laughed at his misery, said, "Who cares?" But I couldn't. Vampires were monsters, but not Drake. At least not right now.

I scooted a little closer to him and stayed seated by his side the rest of night.

LAST NIGHT, THEA STAYED WITH ME FOR HOURS. WE DIDN'T speak. We barely even looked at each other. But for the first time since I had started this ritual hundreds of years ago, I hadn't wanted to be alone.

Close to dawn, we returned to my quarters, and I walked her to her bedroom. I stared at her door for a long while, wondering why I felt such a pull toward her, a pull that tugged deep in my chest, a pull that I couldn't understand.

And now, as the sun set, I was once more staring at her closed door and resisting that pull.

What the hell was happening to me?

I heard her rising from bed and shuffling around her bedroom. Ashamed of my weakness, I scurried to the dining room, where I found my usual bottle and glass of blood.

I downed half the bottle in two seconds.

The moment her bedroom door opened, her scent reached my nose. I guzzled the rest of the bottle. I would have preferred waiting for her to have breakfast together, but I knew she didn't like seeing me drinking blood.

More importantly, I needed to make sure I was in control of my instincts before she got too close.

"Good evening," she said, taking her usual seat at the center of the table.

Desperately, I tried not to stare at her. At how the dark orange and purple rays of the sunset streaming through the window illuminated her fair skin and gave her a smooth, sun-kissed glow. At how the beautiful dark blue dress emphasized the light gray of her eyes, hugged her curves, and showed off her long legs. At how the vein in her neck popped when she glanced at me, and how much it called to me.

"Morning," I forced out.

She narrowed her eyes at me. "Are you okay?"

I cleared my throat. "Of course."

Thomas came in with Thea's breakfast, but to my surprise, she didn't touch it. Instead, she returned her gaze to me. "It has been ten days. The mourning period is over."

I nodded. "Yes. We'll decide on a new leader today."

She cocked her head to the side. "Do you think you'll win?"

"I'm not sure. To be honest, I would rather not. However, if it's Alex or me, then I'll accept the position."

"I hope you win," she said, her words ringing true.

Pride filled my chest, and I cleared my throat. "Please, don't roam the castle for the next couple of hours." The meeting was sure to be tense and difficult. Depending on the results, the other vampires could go crazy and start a rebellion. I didn't want Thea or Thomas out of my protected quarters if that were the case.

She looked disappointed, but said, "I won't."

"Good," was all I said before marching out of my quarters.

While walking to the council room, I pushed all thought

of Thea and the duel out of my mind. I needed to focus on this meeting and nothing else right now—no beautiful Thea, no intoxicating scent, no brilliant hair, no long neck, no wonderful legs.

Groaning, I closed my eyes and focused.

Focus.

The moment I stepped into the council room and saw all the princes in their throne-like chairs and a few of their men standing behind them, I was game. I took my seat with Lewis and Tank already standing behind it. All the while, Alex shot me nasty glances while whispering with Ralf and Eden.

A low growl rose in my chest.

Alex smiled at me.

My hands balled into fists.

Sarki strolled into the room. As she had so many times, she stood beside the bigger chair in the middle of the half circle. Ceremoniously, she stared at the chair, a hand over the dark red velvet back.

She inhaled sharply, and then turned to us. "The mourning period is over," she said, her voice loud and sure. "It's time to choose a new leader."

"What about Alex and Drake's duel?" Dorian asked. He seemed too eager to see us fight.

Sarki turned cold eyes to him. "We have more important matters to attend to right now. We'll talk about the duel later."

"But—"

Sarki snarled. "We'll start with the choosing of a new leader," she barked, interrupting whatever Alex was trying to say.

The room went silent for a heartbeat.

"Did Lord Reynard leave a will?" Cain asked.

"Unfortunately, no," Sarki said. "Because of that, our rules state the princes need to vote." She glanced to Prince Aston first. "Who do you nominate to be our next lord?"

"Alex," he said, no doubt in his voice.

A cold chill ran down my spine.

Sarki continued, going from prince to prince. After much discussion and deadly stares among the princes, Nolan, Dorian, and Patrick voted for Alex; Phelps, Albert, Gray, and Cain voted for me. Of course, Alex voted for himself and as much as it disgusted me, I voted for myself too.

Five votes for Alex, five votes for me.

"It's a tie," Albert said. "It's up to you, Sarki. You'll be the deciding vote."

Her dark eyes glanced from Alex to me. She took a long inhale and finally said, "To be honest, I think we shouldn't choose a new leader before we find Lord Reynard's murderer."

All the princes started talking at once, some indignant about her suggestion, some approving of it.

Finally, I said, "I agree with Sarki." I turned my steely stare to Alex. "What if we end up voting for the killer? We wouldn't want that."

Alex's lips stretched in a malicious grin. "We sure don't want that." He smiled at Sarki. "I agree with you, Sarki. We should find the killer and deal with him before naming a new lord."

"Then, we should start the questioning right away," Sarki suggested.

Alex slouched in his seat, looking pleased. "If I might, I name Prince Drake to be the first one questioned."

I burned a hole in his head with my eyes while he grinned at me.

"Prince Drake?" Sarki asked. I turned my gaze to her. "Can we start?"

I relaxed my shoulders. "Sure. I have nothing to hide."

Sarki stood beside Lord Reynard's chair the entire time the princes questioned me.

"Where were you at the time of the murder?"

What kind of question was that? "In the ballroom with everyone else."

"What did you do when the lights went out?"

"I was holding a wounded human girl and guiding her friend out of the ballroom."

"Why did you want to leave?"

"Because one of the girls was badly hurt."

"What happened to her?"

"She died."

"You killed her?"

"No. She died from the injuries she received during the party, caused by another vampire."

"Do you know who turned off the lights?"

Hell ... "No."

"Do you have reason to believe anyone here would want Lord Reynard dead?"

I glanced to Alex as I answered, "Yes."

"And who is that?"

"Prince Alex."

"Elaborate."

"He has had eyes on Lord Reynard's power for centuries now."

Alex chuckled. "He's saying that because I had my eyes on his pet during the ball."

Red tinted my vision.

"Is that right? Are you accusing Prince Alex because of your blood slave?"

"No!" My voice rose. "Alex and I have never seen eye to eye. Lord Reynard and I had a significant relationship and Alex was jealous."

Alex scoffed. "Jealous? Are you five years old?"

"It's the truth," I said through gritted teeth. "For years you've been trying to steal my missions and my glory. Each time I succeeded, you would play it down, saying you could have done better, or citing some success to try to dilute my victories. When I failed, you stomped all over it, telling Lord Reynard how wrong he was in making me a prince."

He glared at me. "I still think he was wrong."

"Thankfully, it wasn't your decision."

Alex started to rise from his chair, but Sarki shot him a glare. "Control your temper, Prince Alex."

Growling, Alex sat back down, but his body was tense and his gaze screamed murder. Why couldn't the others see he was Reynard's killer? It was written all over his face, all over his actions.

"Everyone here knows your story, Prince Drake," Nolan said as a matter of fact. "You have every reason to hate Lord Reynard."

My nostrils flared.

I had hated the man in the beginning. I had wanted to kill him, to skin him alive, to tie him down in the sunlight and watch him burn, but that had been a long time ago. With time, Lord Reynard proved he wasn't as bad as I wanted him to be and he won me over. Thinking of the past still hurt, but now, I was able to separate those two parts of my life—there was a before and an after being a vampire, and they both were different.

"If that was the case, then why didn't I do it centuries ago? Why wait until now?"

The princes exchanged glances as if trying to come up with a good answer for that. There was none.

"Perhaps you were biding your time," Alex suggested. "You wanted to gain his trust before you took his life."

"If I were that petty, then I would have killed him with the lights turned on so he could see my face while I did it. And again, I won his trust long ago. If I had considered killing Lord Reynard, I wouldn't have waited until now."

"What about your new blood slave, the one that survived?" Aston asked, taking me by surprise.

Why were we talking about her again? She had nothing to do with this. "What about her?"

"Why did you claim her?"

"I fail to see the connection between this question and Lord Reynard's death," I said, controlling my voice so my anger and frustration wouldn't show. Though I bet they could see how angry and frustrated I was by the clench of my fists and the tic in my jaw.

"Lord Reynard never favored humans," Dorian said. "In all my centuries with him, I haven't seen him claim any human blood slaves for himself, and yet, these last two makes how many? Six or seven blood slaves you claimed and took to your quarters?"

I sucked in a sharp breath.

Seven. It made seven. But it was the first time I had taken two young women—and if I was being honest to myself, I only took Judy in because of Thea. Before them, I had taken Thomas because I couldn't stand there and watch an eight-year-old die. As for the other four ... most had been in the same situation as Thomas. Young boys who reminded me of myself. Only one had been an older woman who resembled my mother. I took her in, and after losing her fear of me, she had treated me like her son—a luxury I didn't deserve.

"Lord Reynard didn't take blood slaves. I did. I still fail to see the connection between that and his murder."

"You're a human lover," Aston said. "You prefer humans to your own kind."

"That's ..." I didn't know what to say.

"That is the truth and you know it," Nolan added.

"If it came between a human and a vampire, you would save the human," Dorian said.

"Perhaps Lord Reynard seemed interested in one of your pets, and you wouldn't stand for it," Aston suggest.

"That's absurd!" Gray defended me.

"No, that's the most accurate thing I've heard all night," Alex said, a smug grin across his face.

"Did Lord Reynard show interest in your new pet?" Dorian asked. "What's her name?"

"Thea Harrington," Alex said.

I clenched my fists before I used them to squeeze Alex's throat until his neck broke.

"Did Lord Reynard show any interest in Thea that night?" Dorian asked again.

"No!" I almost shouted, losing my patience. "He didn't come close to her that night, and even if he had showed interest in her, I know he would have backed off after I asked him." I glared at Alex. "Unlike others."

"We might need to question her," Cain suggested. What the hell? He had voted for me, and now he was stabbing me in the back?

My blood boiled. I stood and barked, "The hell you will!

She'll stay in my quarters, and none of you will ever get near her again."

The room went silent for a moment, and then it burst into a swarm of harsh words and whispers. The princes talked among themselves, deciding my future.

My insides tensed, because no matter what had happened, I knew the outcome I would have to face here.

Prince Aston rose to his feet and said, "Prince Drake, your questioning is over for now." He paused. "After hearing your answers, we've concluded you're a suspect in Lord Reynard's death."

17

THEA

DRAKE HAD BEEN GONE FOR HOURS, AND I WAS CRAWLING THE walls inside his chambers. I loved reading and the place had everything I needed, but I also needed fresh air. Besides, I had to roam the castle. There was no choice here.

When I proposed to Thomas that we go out for a stroll, he freaked out, reminding me Drake had asked us to stay inside.

"That was hours ago," I protested. "I'm going, with or without you."

For a moment, I wished he would stay so I would be able to go around the castle without having to lie to him. To my surprise, he grumbled but came with me.

However, once we got to the garden, another young slave appeared and asked Thomas to help with something. Thomas seemed unsure about me. He wanted to take me back inside before going to help, but after I promised to stay put and wait for him in the gardens, he finally followed the other slave out.

And I was alone in the gardens.

My first instinct was to run inside the castle and continue

my search, but the dread about bumping into other vampires was too big. I had been lucky so far, I knew that, and I wasn't sure how long I could push it.

But I had to try. I had to go. I had to find it.

I would, but after I spent some time outside and took lungfuls of fresh air. I missed being outside.

Taking a deep breath, I glanced at the moon and admired its glow. I had always thought I liked the moon more than the sun, as if the moon and I had a connection or something.

But now, after being locked inside the castle for ten days, I realized I liked the sun too. I missed it like crazy. I missed the brightness, the colors, and the sounds of the world in daylight.

I chose a secluded corner outside the maze and sat down on a stone bench, flirting with the moon and the stars.

How was I going to amble around the castle without being seen? How was I going to search its dark corners if Thomas was supposed to be with me all the time? And when he wasn't, I risked being found out by a less than friendly vampire. Besides, I was sure I was wasting my time searching in such obvious places.

I sighed.

Wherever it was hidden, it would probably take more than sneaking around to retrieve it.

"Hell …"

I stilled as the faint voice reached my ears. My heart sped as I thought about what to do. Stay here and hope whoever it was didn't come this way, or hide in the maze and hope the vampire didn't smell me from a mile away? Neither were great solutions.

I rose and settled on hiding in the maze. But, before I could take a step, Drake appeared right in front me.

"Holy ..." I fell back on the bench, my hand over my racing heart. "You scared me!"

He stepped back. "I apologize."

I took a deep breath, trying to slow down my pulse. My gaze, though, wouldn't leave Drake. I had thought he looked imposing in a black suit, white shirt, and burgundy tie before leaving his chambers earlier tonight, but now, under the moonlight and among the dark shrubs of the garden? He looked like an actor ready to rock the red carpet.

My heart sped up again.

However, his expression was different. Usually, he stared at me with indifference, only showing the briefest of emotions here and there. Tonight, his green eyes were dull and his shoulders were sagged.

"What's wrong?" I asked before I could think it through. "What happened at the meeting?" My insides coiled. "Don't tell me Alex won."

Drake ran a hand through his hair, pushing the long strands out of his beautiful face. "No, no one won. It was a tie and we turned to Sarki to decide, but she suggested we find Lord Reynard's killer first."

"And?"

"A questioning started, and I was the first in line."

"So you cleared your name." I was certain he hadn't done it. Even with his super strength and speed, he had been right by my side the entire time. He couldn't have done it.

Drake sat down on the bench beside me and exhaled through his nose. "No. Actually, I'm on the line as one of the suspects."

"Why?"

He turned his solemn eyes to me. "Because I defended you."

A shock ran through my core. "W-what? Why?"

"Because they think I favor humans over vampires, and since Reynard wasn't fond of humans, they think I killed him to protect you."

"That ... that makes no sense. You hadn't claimed me for five minutes before Lord Reynard was killed, and he didn't even know me. He hadn't shown interest in me. You had no reason to kill him."

"That's exactly what I told them, but it seems Alex has half of the princes under his thumb. He throws out a lie and the others spin it out of proportion."

"That's crazy. What happens now?"

"They interrogated all the princes and decided three of us had reasons to kill Lord Reynard. Alex, Cain, and me. Now the three of us will be investigated. In about a week, we'll be interrogated again, and hopefully by then, they will have found the culprit."

I shook my head. "What if the killer isn't any of you three? What if whoever did it is hiding it well?"

"I know. I thought about that."

"Can't you use compulsion to extract the truth?"

"It doesn't work as well from vampire to vampire. The stronger the vampire, the weaker the compulsion will be. For example, Lord Reynard was so old and powerful, no compulsion worked on him. None of ours anyway."

I stared out to the fountain in the distance, thinking, considering. There had to be a way to clear Drake's name. It wasn't fair he was incriminated for something he didn't do.

And why was I trying to defend a vampire? All vampires were monsters.

Weren't they?

I returned my gaze to Drake and found him staring at me.

Like this, when his expression was downcast, he looked almost human. Almost. He was too handsome, too stunning to be a simple human.

"Why did you claim me?" The question rolled off my tongue without my consent.

His brows dipped and his lips pressed into a thin line. I thought he wouldn't answer, until he finally said, "I saw you there in the middle of the ballroom, holding a girl you barely knew with all you had, and fighting vampires as if you had any chance of winning."

My cheeks warmed in embarrassment. "Thank you for the vote of confidence."

One corner of his lips curled up. "Don't get me wrong. I thought it was amazing. It seems you know how to fight, which is great, but unfortunately, that won't do much good against vampires."

"It was all I could think of doing in the moment."

"I know, and I admire you for it," he said, his rough voice sprinkled with a soft undertone. "Anyway, seeing you there, fighting for her, fighting for yourself ... I don't know what came over me."

"Despite my anger in the beginning, I want to thank you." I suppressed a shudder. "I know now I could have ended up with a much worse fate."

"You're welcome," he said in a low voice.

I felt like Sherlock Holmes trying to solve a mystery. "We need to think of a way to prove your innocence."

"I appreciate the help, but if they want to blame me, nothing will stop them, not even if the truth hits them in the face."

"That's crazy. They can't do that."

"They can and they will. They'll use you and my past,

spin an absurd tale about how it all connects, and use it against me."

The words itched in my throat, and I tried holding them back. "Your past?"

He looked up at the moon and its glow illuminated only half of his face, creating shadows that emphasized his sharp nose, his full mouth, and the sharp edges of his chin and jaw. My eyes followed the line of his jaw down the smooth skin of his long neck.

I swallowed hard, incapable of pushing down the feelings stirring inside me. Drake was a vampire. He was a monster.

"My family and I were happy," he started, his voice rough. "At least, that's how I remember it. We weren't rich, but we lived well for that time. I was the oldest of four children, and my parents were good parents. I remember Father getting mad at us when we misbehaved, but other than a few slaps on our bottoms and having extra chores here and there, he was good to us." His gaze turned to the imposing castle bathed in moonlight. "Our village was attacked by vampires when I was sixteen. They invaded my home and killed my family right in front of me. When they came for me, I fought, much like you did that night at the ball. I fought with all I had, and to my surprise, I was doing quite well. But then the leader of the vampires saw me fighting, and he was quite impressed with my ability. He took me on as his pupil, as he used to say. I hated him. I wanted to kill him. I plotted how to sneak into his suite and kill him so many times. But he treated me well. He took care of me. He raised me. He taught me politics, he showed me what his army did, what they fought for, he taught me how to fight. I still hated vampires with all my soul, but this man, this vampire ... he was different. I started not hating him, and then, on my twenty-fifth birthday, he turned me."

I reached over and placed my hand on his. "I'm sorry." It was the only thing I could think to say.

"I was too. I think I still am. At first, my old hate consumed me. I rebelled. I left. I spent many years alone and even considered ending my life. But ..." He sighed. "I couldn't do it. I thought about my parents and my siblings, about how I would have wanted them to live—not as vampires, but as humans. I wanted them to live long, happy lives, and because of that guilt, I couldn't do it. I've always hated being a vampire, but I can't undo it, and I couldn't take my own life. So, I came back to my maker and I joined his army. I became his right hand."

I gasped as his words sank in. "Lord Reynard," I whispered. "Lord Reynard killed your family. He took you as a blood slave. Then he turned you." I couldn't believe it. "And you still stuck with him?"

He let out a hollow chuckle. "I know it doesn't make much sense, but when you live for so long, some things, some grudges start to seem petty. You let go of them." His brows furrowed. "But not everything. Never everything."

"That's why they suspect you. Because Lord Reynard killed your family."

"Yes."

I slid my hand up his arm. "I'm sorry." I felt the muscles of his arm stiffen. His gaze dipped to my hand and a knot appeared between his brows. "I'm sorry for your family. I'm sorry you had to live as a blood slave to the man you hated. I'm sorry you're a suspect in the death of the man you came to love."

His eyes fixed on mine, a glint in them I didn't want to

recognize, but couldn't ignore. Couldn't because I was feeling something similar.

Drake placed his hand over mine, the intensity of his eyes taking my breath away. "Thea ..."

"Yes?" I asked, my throat dry.

"You ... I'm ..." His gaze fell on my mouth and his jaw ticked. "I'm about to do something you might not like," he said, his voice breathy.

Like a bee drawn to a flower, I leaned closer. "Who said I won't like it?"

A deep growl came from his throat before his hand wrapped around my wrist. He tugged me closer. He bent over me. I held my breath. Then he stopped, leaving only half an inch between our lips. His eyes searched mine, as if trying to find any objection in them. He wouldn't find any. Another growl came from him and then his mouth was on mine.

His lips were cold and warm, hard and soft, and his kiss was pure pleasure that moved against me, within me. There was nothing slow about his lips on mine. No, there was only desperate need. He took without asking, and I gave it without hesitating.

His hands traveled around my waist and splayed on my back, pushing me closer, and I held on to his shoulders, afraid this was all but a dream. A deliciously impossible dream.

Surprising me, Drake pulled back, his face stricken. "I'm sorry. That was wrong. I shouldn't have done that. You—"

"Drake." I grabbed his shirt and tugged him back to me. "Just shut up and kiss me."

One corner of his lips curled up before his mouth descended on mine again.

18

DRAKE

I PACED THE HALLWAY, UP AND DOWN, UP AND DOWN. THE restlessness in me was ridiculous. Every feeling inside me right now was ridiculous. I had no idea I could feel like this. Like I wanted to be beside someone every second of every day, like I would do anything, *anything*, to protect her, like my life didn't matter, didn't have any meaning, before I met her.

I felt like I was a fifteen-year-old human again—stupid and easily taken over by hormones.

This was ridiculous.

Stupid and ridic—

The door of her suite opened and I halted. Thea stepped out, wearing another summer dress that showed too much of her smooth, silky skin.

My breath caught.

She glanced at me, a rosy tint rising up her cheeks. "Hi."

Images from last night flooded my mind, and my body's temperature went up a million degrees. Stopping kissing her had been hard. Almost impossible. It took all of my control not to slip into her bedroom with her and claim more than her freedom.

I had wanted her like I had never wanted anything else in my entire long life. I *still* wanted her.

She batted her lashes, the pink in her cheeks increasing. "Everything okay?"

"Everything is great," I said with a growl. Fast like a cat, I lunged for her. She let out a gasp as I wrapped my hands over her waist and pressed her against the wall. "Everything is perfect." I leaned into her, slow enough to give her time to object, but not too slow or I might explode with the tension building inside me.

She rose to her tiptoes and pressed her lips on mine. A growl started in my chest, but it died when I closed my mouth over hers.

Her lips were warm and soft and tasted like mint and heaven. I didn't deserve heaven, never had, but I couldn't stop now. I needed this heaven; I needed her heaven.

I stepped into her, pinning her to the wall and gluing every inch of my body to hers. She let out a sound that was a mix of a whimper and a moan, a sound that rocked through me, and I almost lost it.

Her scent, her blood rushing, her heart racing, it was too much and too little. I needed more of her, and I needed it right now.

To hell with the hunger that quaked my muscles and demanded a taste of her delicious blood. I wouldn't succumb to it. Thea was more important than that.

Her stomach growled, a faint sound she probably only felt instead of heard, but with my vampire senses, it had been loud enough. I chuckled against her lips. "Someone is hungry." I started pulling back, but she only wound her arms around my neck tighter.

"It can wait," she whispered before deepening the kiss again.

Hell ...

I was a goner. I let her take over for a moment. Surprising me, she ran her tongue over my lower lip before sucking it hard. My gut contracted, and I pushed her harder against the wall, until she felt what she was doing to me.

Her gasp turned into a moan as she readjusted her hips, rubbing more of her on me.

Holy hell. My knees wavered and—

Her stomach growled again.

I stepped back, letting go of her. Thea wobbled to the side, as if she were dizzy, but before I could reach for her again, she slapped her hands on the wall behind her and steadied herself.

There was only three feet between us, but the tension, the heavy charge in the air around us, was palpable. Her eyes met mine, and I could swear the hallway would catch on fire any minute now.

Clearing my throat, I straightened my shirt. Then, I offered her my arm. "Come on. Let's get you some breakfast."

Thea hooked her hand under my arm and smiled at me. "I could have gone longer without breakfast, you know."

An urge to spin her around and pin her to the wall again hit me hard, but I pushed it away. I had already had breakfast —more blood than I usually had at this time, just to be safe— but she hadn't. As a human, she was way more fragile than I was.

Besides, taking her to breakfast gave me a break. It would force me away from her, and this way I could think clearly—

something I didn't have any control over when she was so close.

In the dining room, Thea let go of my arm and took her usual seat at the middle of the table. I fought the pull to take the seat beside her, because I really needed to think straight, and sat at the end of the table.

Her brow furrowed, Thea looked at the food spread in front of her.

"Is there something wrong?"

"No," she said, her voice tight.

In silence, she ate while I thought, though my eyes were on her the entire time.

I had to find a way to prove I was innocent. If I was charged, I would be executed, and then Thea and Thomas would be taken as blood slaves by other vampires. No doubt Alex would claim Thea.

Rage swept over me, and I closed my hands into tight fists.

That couldn't happen.

But if it came to that, then I should have a plan B. I needed to find a way of taking Thea and Thomas away from the palace in case I was killed. But how?

I heard the shuffling outside the door two seconds before a knock sounded loud and clear.

Her eyes wide, Thea straightened in her chair.

"It's okay," I assured her, standing up. "It's only Holden, one of my guards."

Thomas beat me to the door. He took a sealed envelope from Holden, then delivered it to me.

Thomas helped clear Thea's breakfast while I opened the letter and read it. A quick note from Gray, asking me to meet him in his quarters.

I approached Thea, who was watching from the steps

before the dining room. "I have to go out for a bit," I told her. I glanced at Thomas, who was across the room. "Things aren't going well around the castle, so, please, you two stay inside today."

"Yes, my prince," Thomas said with a slight bow of his head. I had already told him over a hundred times to stop calling me that and bowing to me, but he kept doing it.

Thea's brows knotted. "Are you okay?"

A soft smile tugged at my lips and pride bloomed in my chest at the worry in her voice. "I think so. I'm going talk to another prince. As far as I know, he's on my side."

"Be careful," she whispered.

I leaned into her and pressed my lips in her forehead. "Always." More now than ever.

Without another glance or words, I dashed out of my chambers, probably faster than Thea's and Thomas' eyes could follow.

I hated leaving her, but it was probably for the best. I needed some fresh air, even if it was visiting another corner of the castle where her sweet scent wasn't filling every square inch.

The guards in front of Gray's chambers saw me approaching and opened the front door for me. They lowered their heads when I walked by them and stepped inside.

Prince Gray and Prince Phelps were seated on the long, black leather sofa in the center of the living room. Unlike my place, the other princes liked to follow the castle's decoration —dark walls, dark floors, dark furniture, with black and deep red predominating over browns and dark gray.

"Prince Drake, take a seat," Gray said.

Reluctantly, I sat down in a heavy armchair across from the sofa. "What is this about?"

"Since we're on your side," Phelps started, "we felt the need to tell you Prince Alex has been active since the interrogations last night. He has been going from prince to prince, trying to get them all on his side."

I gritted my teeth. Of course he was. "What else do you know?"

"Not much," Gray said. "He approached us, told us some lies about you, and Lord Reynard, and your new pet." A waved of anger rolled in my stomach. Thea was not my pet. I wasn't sure what she was yet, but she definitely meant a lot. "He's even spreading rumors to lower-ranking vampires, in the hopes that it'll cause paranoia in everyone in the castle."

"He's doing whatever he can to incriminate you," Phelps added.

"Hell," I muttered, running a hand through my hair.

"Besides all that," Gray said, "we just received a report from one of our informants that some witch covens are on the move. They are agitated. We think they know we're uncentered now that Lord Reynard is gone, and we haven't chosen a new lord yet. They might take advantage of that and attack."

"Which will lead to a full out war," Phelps said.

I grunted under my breath. Witches were vile, petty beings. They took advantage of every situation they could, and these witches wouldn't be any different. We all knew the stories of witches taking over powerful vampire covens and werewolves packs all over the world—and all they had to do was wait for the right opportunity.

"We need to find the real killer and fast," I said, the wheels in my head turning in rapid succession. "And then we need to elect a new leader."

"Exactly," Gray said. "The longer we wait, the more chances the witches will have to strike."

Holy hell ... "If Alex isn't playing fair, then we shouldn't either," I said. "We can't wait until everything crumbles to dust. We need to act now."

Phelps let out a long breath. "Do you have any ideas?"

I groaned, feeling hopeless. "Not one."

19

THEA

I KNEW IT WAS A DREAM, BUT IT WAS A DAMN GOOD ONE.

Drake slipped into bed with me, and staring with dark, hungry eyes, he ripped my nightgown to pieces, revealing my naked body underneath. Then, he lowered himself over me, pressing his hard body on mine, and his delicious mouth against mine.

I half-sighed and half-moaned as—

A scream filled the night, and I jerked up, awake and alert.

That hadn't come from my dream, I was sure.

Holding my breath, I waited.

The scream echoed through my bedroom again.

I darted off the bed, grabbed a thin robe, and tied it over myself while I ran into the corridor. I bumped into Thomas.

"Was that you?" he asked, his eyes wide.

"No," I said, my heart racing.

If it wasn't him, or me, then ...

The scream came again, more guttural and low this time.

My heart sank. "Drake."

Thomas and I ran to the prince's suite at the end of the hallway.

Thomas pushed the door open, and we both skidded to a stop at the sight inside. Like that night in the ballroom, Drake was pinned to the wall by two long swords protruding through his shoulders, and a thick wooden stake in his chest.

My hand flew to my mouth. "Oh my ..."

Drake growled, a scream lost in his throat.

Thomas and I rushed to him, and with some effort, we pulled the swords out. Drake slumped to the floor, his fall cushioned by my weak hold on his heavy body. With effort, we laid him down, his head on my legs.

"Is he ...?" Thomas asked, his huge eyes darting from the stake in Drake's chest to my face.

My hand hovered over the stake as I examined it. "I don't think so. I think ... I think the stake missed his heart."

As if to confirm he wasn't dead, Drake's eyes fluttered open and his unfocused gaze met mine. "Thea," he whispered, his voice weak.

"Shh," I whispered back as tears clouded my vision. I had just admitted to myself how much I liked him, how much I was willing to see where this was going. He couldn't die now. I pulled the top comforter from the bed and pressed a corner of it around the stake, trying to stop the bleeding. "Save your strength."

Kneeling beside us, Thomas fidgeted, his body rocking front and back, as if he needed the motion to control himself. "What do we do? What do we do?"

I racked my brain. "We shouldn't take the stake out, not yet. It might do more harm than good. We also shouldn't move him, in case the stake moves with him and reaches his heart." I traced my fingertips over Drake's sweaty and feverish face. "We need a healer. Go fetch a healer from the infirmary."

Thomas shook his head. "No, that's dangerous. Most men there love Prince Alex. They might betray us."

"Then who? Who can we trust? Who can heal him?"

"Sarki," Thomas said. "She always favored Prince Drake and she's half witch. She might be able to heal him."

"Then go!" I hissed. "Bring her here. Fast."

Thomas skidded out of the bedroom, his footfalls dull on the cold floor.

I ran my hand over Drake's face once more, pushing his hair away from his forehead.

"Thea," he whispered. He blinked, trying to look at me.

"Be quiet, Drake," I told him, my voice gentle. "You need to conserve your strength."

A half smile appeared over his pale lips. "I appreciate the concern, but I'm afraid I'm too far gone."

I shook my head hard. "Don't say that. Don't you dare say that. Fight, Drake. Please, I beg you, fight."

His eyes fluttered open and he stared at me. "I had so much to tell you."

Tears burned behind my eyes. "You will tell me all of it. Because I need you to." I took his hand in mine and brought it to my face. "Please, for me, fight."

A snarl rumbled his chest as if pain ricocheted through his body.

For a few long minutes, Drake seemed to shift in and out of consciousness, his fever increasing and his body trembling in shock. Praying to all the gods and goddesses out there, I sang a lullaby my mother used to sing to me when I had a nightmare or was too sick and couldn't sleep.

Finally, Thomas and Sarki joined me in Drake's bedroom.

Sarki's dark complexion gained a pale tint as she stared at Drake's wounds. "What the ...?"

"Sarki, please, use your magic and heal him," I asked, a pleading tone to my voice.

She padded toward us, visibly shocked. "I-I can't." She knelt beside me, her wide gaze on Drake. "I'm only half-witch. My magic is weak. I can't perform healing spells."

My heart sank along with any hope.

Unless ...

My secret be damned. If I could heal Drake and they found out about it, so be it. I wasn't going to let Drake die.

"Can you make potions?"

She stared at me. "W-what?"

"Can you use your magic to make potions?" I asked again.

"Yes, but the only healing potions I know are salves, which only help with superficial cuts and diminish pain. I don't know any potion for a wound of this magnitude."

"I do," I said, aware of Sarki's and Thomas's curious gazes. "We'll need valerian, white sage, woad, multein, and witch's bark, a mortar and pestle, and a spoon or glass. Can you find those for me?"

"I know there are mortar and pestles in the kitchen," Thomas said. "I can get one."

"And there should be all those herbs in the infirmary," Sarki said. "I'll be back in a few minutes."

"Hurry!" I told them as they ran out.

I counted the minutes, pretending Drake's tremors lessened and his breathing slowed. He didn't even try opening his eyes anymore.

I swallowed the terror building in my throat. Now wasn't

the time for despair. Now was the time for action. All I needed was for Thomas and Sarki to be back.

To make things worse, we had no idea who did this. It could have been anyone. They had entered Drake's chambers undetected and simply—I sucked in a sharp breath, pushing the images of Drake pinned to the wall from my mind.

I glanced around the room, praying whoever had tried to kill Drake wasn't lurking in the shadows, waiting to finish what he had started.

As a precaution, I reached under Drake's pillow and pulled the dagger from under it. I kept it close to my side in case I needed to defend our lives.

It took them a while, but finally Sarki and Thomas came back with all we needed. While Thomas swept through the chambers to make sure we were safe now, I instructed Sarki on how to make the potion—which herbs to crush first, the quantity, the order, when to apply her magic, and what kind of spell she needed. She did it all without questioning how I knew all of this.

When the herbs became a thick, dark blue potion and it bubbled without the need for fire, I told her to stop. I grabbed the spoon Thomas had brought, dipped it into the potion, and fed a spoonful to Drake's mouth.

As the thick liquid went down his throat, he coughed and tried to spit it out. I placed my hand over his mouth. "Swallow it. I know it tastes bad and the texture doesn't help, but please swallow it."

I didn't think he was hearing anything at the moment, but as I poured more of the potion into his mouth, he started swallowing—and gagging.

"That should be enough," I said, after ten spoonfuls.

The three of us watched Drake with hawk eyes.

"I don't see anything," Thomas said, his voice breaking.

"Wait," I said, praying it had worked. Praying it would work. "His wound is deep. It might take a while." At least, I hoped that was the only problem.

Finally, after what seemed like an eternity, the stake was pushed out and Drake's wounds started closing.

I let out a relieved sigh and content tears filled my eyes. I smiled at Sarki and Thomas, and found they looked as relieved as I felt.

Another long moment passed and Drake groaned. His eyes fluttered open and he glanced at me. "What happened?"

"You don't remember?" I asked, running my hand over his face. I felt the need to touch him, to feel his chest rising with each breath he took, to see the color returning to his beautiful face.

"I ..." He pushed up and groaned, his hand going to his chest. His eyes widened. "I was pinned to the wall, like Reynard was."

"Prince Drake," Thomas started. "Did you see who did it?"

Drake frowned, thinking. "No. I was sleeping, then I was pulled up and pinned to the wall. Everything happened too fast, in the dark, and I had been half asleep."

"You didn't even catch a scent?" Sarki asked.

He shook his head. "I ... Like I said, I was half asleep. I remember too many scents, but half are probably from my dreams." He glanced from Thomas, to Sarki, to me. "Wait ..." He glanced down at his shirt and the floor, soaked in red blood. "How am I alive now?"

A wide smile took over Sarki's lips. "It was all Thea's doing. She knew exactly how to heal you." I couldn't tell if she was being sarcastic or curious, but right now, I didn't care. All that mattered was that Drake was fine.

"What did you do?" Drake asked, a hint of wonder in his voice.

I shrugged. "I was always curious and studied Wicca. I learned a potion or two."

I ignored Sarki's heated stare, one that told me she knew I wouldn't have been able to find the recipe for a healing potion like that in a random book at the library.

"Are you okay, Prince Drake?" Thomas asked.

Drake took a long breath. "I think so. Thank you for your help, Thomas. You too, Sarki."

"My pleasure." Sarki pushed up to her feet. "Since you're okay, I'll return to my chambers. It's still the middle of the day, and I have a long night ahead of me." She waved us goodbye and sauntered out of the bedroom like a top model on a catwalk.

After some more questions of "are you sure you're alright?" Thomas shuffled out of bedroom, closing the door behind him.

Once alone, Drake took my hand and stood, pulling me with him. He held my hand tight and stared down at me, his eyes with a new shine. "I have no idea how you did it, but thank you."

Swallowing hard, I took a step back. Rumors would spread, even though I hoped Thomas and Sarki didn't tell anyone about it. But, once Drake was well enough and thought about it, he would know something was amiss. He would put two and two together. He would probably feel betrayed and question me.

Better if I told him the truth myself. "I have something to tell you," I forced out.

He lifted an eyebrow, proving to me the healing potion had really worked and he was doing well already. "What is it?"

I sucked in a sharp breath, sure he would hate me with my next words. "I'm a witch."

20

I couldn't have heard her right.

My instinct kicked in and I took a large step back. "What?"

Thea's cheeks gained a flustered tint. "I'm a witch."

That didn't make sense. How was she a witch? If she were, she wouldn't have been chosen to come to the castle. We screened everyone who applied for an invitation and only picked the best candidates.

"That can't be true," I said, my words echoing what thrummed in my mind.

"It is." She sighed. "Many years before I was born, Lord Reynard had trouble with a few witch covens: the Black-marsh, the Bluemoon, and the Silverblood. He attacked Silverblood first, taking the witches by surprise. And he stole the heart of the coven. Do you know what that means?"

"The heart of the first witch from the coven," I said, knowing well. "The witch may die, but her heart is kept alive, beating inside a chest. The heart is supposed to stay close to the coven, usually inside a sanctuary, otherwise the witches lose their powers."

"Exactly. Lord Reynard stole the heart of the Silverblood coven. When he turned to the Blackmarsh and Bluemoon, they were prepared. They ran with the hearts of their covens and kept them safe."

I nodded. "I remember that. I was involved with some werewolf business up north, but I remember hearing about it. It was about fifty years ago, maybe? Lord Reynard came back to the castle and showed the heart to all of us as if it were a trophy."

Thea pressed her lips tight. "That's the heart of my coven." I sucked in a sharp breath. Oh, hell ... "For fifty years, the witches in my coven have been weakening. I was born weak. We did what we could, using potions when spells wouldn't do, but some covens crave war and blood. Blackmarsh know we're weakening. We think they know our heart was taken, and they plan on attacking us." She paused, staring at me with a harsh glint in her eyes. "They plan on attacking my coven, my family. And, without the heart, there isn't much we can do to protect ourselves."

It was like the pieces of the puzzle suddenly fit together. "You're here to retrieve the heart."

She nodded. "We've been trying to get in here for many years."

"But ... how? We wouldn't let witches in."

"We have resources. Besides, we're weakening, but our magic isn't all gone. In a last attempt, we used a lot of it to trick the system, as you said, and get me invited in."

Though it was a suicidal plan, and a little crazy, I had to agree it was also genius. "Why you?"

"Because I'm young and still have a little magic. Not enough to make a powerful healing spell, though."

I hated witches, always had. They were a miserable, insufferable bunch who only liked to stir trouble and take advantage of everyone. I wanted to hate Thea. But she was doing what she had to do to keep her family safe. She was putting her life at great risk for a mission she was likely to fail, but she was their only hope. More importantly, she had saved me. She didn't need to do that, but she risked Sarki and Thomas finding out what she really was to save me. If she hadn't been here, if she hadn't come to this castle, I would be dead by now.

"But ... you could have been killed during the feast."

"We took that part into consideration when devising a plan." She fished a thumbnail-sized brooch from the inside of her nightgown's collar. "I've been using this, because it makes my scent undesirable to vampires. They wouldn't push me away, but they wouldn't attack me either. That was how I planned on surviving the feast and being placed with the other blood slaves. Until you claimed me."

That brooch was supposed to make her scent bad? How come it didn't work for me?

"That's why you like to roam around the castle," I said, realizing the truth. "You've been looking for the heart."

"In vain, though. I'm sure it'll be hidden somewhere I can't reach." She bit her lower lip, her bright gray eyes shining. "I know you must hate me now, but I beg you. If you know where it is, please, tell me."

"You know your mission is suicidal, right? Even if you can get to the heart, how do you plan to escape? It's impossible."

"Once I have the heart, my magic should increase. It'll probably be hard, but as long as I make it outside, another witch from my coven would come and take the heart from me."

I sucked in a sharp breath. "So you did come to die?"

She lifted her chin. "If that's what it takes, yes, I came knowing it's unlikely I'll walk out alive."

"That's crazy," I muttered, pacing in front of her.

"Please, Drake, if you know where the heart is, tell me."

"I don't know where it is."

"You don't know, or you don't want to tell me?"

Frowning, I halted in front of her. "If I knew, what would you do? Go there now, pick it up, and run."

She stared at me for a moment. "Something like that."

I shook my head, feeling betrayed. Not only because she hid who she was from me, but because she was willing to die for her coven. What about me? Didn't she consider that? Did she think I wanted her to die? Or to run away and never look back?

"I don't know where it is," I repeated.

Her shoulders sagged. "And I'm guessing you won't let me roam the castle anymore to search for it."

Hell ... What now? Was I supposed to keep her as a prisoner inside my quarters? Or inside her bedroom? I couldn't do that to her. Though it hurt me, I understood what she was doing. I might have a problem with all supernatural beings—vampires, witches, werewolves, and the others—but that didn't mean I wanted them gone. I just wanted peace between all the covens and packs and species.

"With the investigation into Reynard's death, the castle is on high alert. It won't do any good for you to roam around. In fact, I want you and Thomas inside my quarters at all times."

"But—"

"I'll look for the heart for you."

Tears filled her wide eyes. "You would do that?"

The hope in her voice cut through my heart. I couldn't deny it anymore. I cared about her too much. It didn't matter if she was a witch or if she was planning on leaving me soon. As long as she was safe and well, I would be okay. And to make sure she continued to be safe, I would have to help her.

I took a step toward her. "I would do anything for you."

A muffled sob caught in her throat, and a tear slid down her cheeks. "Thank you," she whispered.

I cupped her face and wiped the tear away. "Don't thank me yet." I wound my arm around her waist and pulled her into me. I had to feel her body against mine, her heart thumping and vibrating under my hand. I wanted to wrap her around me and keep her for eternity.

That realization took my breath away.

I wasn't falling for her. I had already fallen.

Surrendering to the pull inside my chest and the raw desire in my heart, I leaned into her and kissed her.

21

THEA

THERE WAS NOTHING BETTER IN THIS WORLD THAN KISSING Drake.

I confess that when I told him I was a witch, I had expected him to rage and yell and maybe even throw me out, to go live with the other blood slaves, or to be taken by whoever crossed my path first.

Most likely Alex.

I shuddered at the thought, but then Drake's tongue swept over my lips and I lost my mind. My mind and my heart.

Vampires were monsters, but Drake was different. He had a good heart. If he led Castle DuMoir, maybe things would change, and the witches wouldn't hate vampires so much. If he became the new Lord, maybe he would let me walk out with my coven's heart, but that wouldn't be the end for us.

Because I really didn't want it to end.

I had come in here sure I was going to die, one way or another. I was supposed to retrieve the heart and hand it back to the coven. If I died in the process, I had been okay with that, because it was my duty. I would die with honor. Doing what was right.

But now, with Drake's soft lips pressed against mine, moving in a frantic rhythm, as if I were the moonlight of his existence … now I wasn't so sure I wanted to die.

Taking my breath away, Drake spun us around with his super speed, and pinned me to the wall. Without breaking the kiss, he glued his hard body to mine and ran his hands down my hips.

His mouth wandered from my mouth to my chin, and he bit the soft spot between my shoulder and neck. On instinct, I threw my head back and moaned, digging my nails into his shoulders. I felt when his fangs elongated and he grazed them over my skin.

A sliver of fear snaked through my chest, but then he whispered, "Don't worry. I won't bite you."

He didn't give me time to process his words. He grabbed my ass and pulled me up. Instantly, I wound my legs around his waist. The skirt of my nightgown rode up, and I wiggled, adjusting against him, rubbing on him, making him even harder for me.

His chest rumbled with a growl as he slipped his fingers between us and rubbed through my underwear. Heat and lust traveled through me, and I moaned, my back arching. He moved his mouth from my shoulder to my cleavage, dragging his tongue on the curve of my breasts while his finger inched under my panties. I shivered as he touched my center.

"Please," I whispered. The feelings, the sensations zipping through me … I never thought I was the kind to beg, but right now, I would beg. "Please."

Finally, Drake slipped a finger inside me and I stilled. For a brief moment, all I could do was pant. Then, my hands tightened around his shoulders, and I pulled him to me. He slid a second finger inside me and rubbed my clit with his thumb. Whimpering, I ground my hips in rhythm with his hand.

It didn't take long for my body to start tensing, my hips shifting, my nails digging so hard into his skin I was sure I would have drawn blood if he weren't a vampire. I was so, so close.

"Like this?" he whispered before taking my mouth again. He kissed me even harder and deeper than before, ripping little moans out of me. Drake increased the pressure of his thumb and thrust his fingers faster. "Show me how much you like this."

Eyes closed, I threw my head back, whimpered, tensed, and then broke into little trembles in his arms. I melted, my legs dropping down hard, and if it weren't for his arms around me, I would have slipped to the floor.

Drake held me close and brushed back a strand of my hair from my face. "Are you okay?"

Floating in paradise, I smiled at him. "I'm more than okay."

"We're not done yet." He leaned into me and took my mouth with his. His hands worked to open and push down my nightgown.

With a low growl, Drake pushed me onto the bed, but instead of joining me, he stepped back and looked at me. Just looked at me. His gaze traveled over every inch of my body, his green eyes brewing like a storm. I felt like I should be self-conscious and embarrassed, but then I realized I didn't have a reason to be. I liked the hunger in his eyes, the way they darkened while his whole stance changed, the way his jaw worked, the way he licked his lips as if I was the most beautiful thing he had ever seen.

"You're stunning," he said, his voice husky. I hadn't thought he would say it out loud, and it took me by surprise. "You're too damn gorgeous."

Slowly, he inched to the bed. Dipping his knees, one leg on each side of me, he leaned into me. He ran a finger up my body, sending a blazing fire wherever he touched—my thigh, my hip, my waist, the curve of my breast.

A moan slipped from my throat, and I arched my back into his touch, amazed at how my body reacted to him.

Drake groaned and closed his mouth around my breast. Crying out, I buried my hands in his hair as if to hold him there, because I would die if he moved his mouth away. He teased. He licked. He sucked. He drove me insane with pent up ecstasy. I needed more. I needed him.

"Please ..." I croaked, out of breath.

He growled and lifted his head, his eyes meeting mine. The desire in them, the want ... I shivered, anticipating the moment he was inside me. I couldn't wait.

"What do you want?" he asked.

"You," I said, no hesitation. "You and me. You inside me."

With a satisfied grin, Drake shrugged off his clothes and crawled over me. I barely had time to appreciate the view— he was the gorgeous one with a long, hard body, and a thousand muscles I wanted to explore—as he rested his body over mine and took my mouth with his. I gasped as he plunged his tongue past my lips and claimed me. Wanting more, needing more, I opened my mouth wide, giving him full access.

He positioned myself between my parted legs. I broke the kiss and sucked in a sharp breath as he slid inside me.

"Oh ..." I whimpered as he buried himself deep and stilled, giving me time to get used to him, to how he filled me up, to how I was about to explode with heat and lust and need.

He growled then started moving. Slowly at first. I savored each rub of him against me. It was too much and it still wasn't enough. I clasped his ass and pulled him into me, hoping he would get the hint. He did. With a growl, he pounded into me, taking from me as much as he could. I arched my back, and he wound his arm around my waist, keeping me close. He grazed his tongue across my mouth, my chin, jaw, neck, shoulder, and down my breasts. He clasped a hand around one while sliding his hot tongue along the curve of the other. Lost in the millions of sensations racing under my skin, I moaned, arching my back more and more. Like I had done before, I buried my hands in his hair and held him against me. He teased me, flicking his tongue around my breast, then my nipple, all the while thrusting into me, hard and deep. I cried out in pain and pleasure. He sucked on my nipple, then he opened his mouth and took as much of my breast as he could. I cried out again.

"Hell," he whispered against my skin.

Boldness surged through me. I pushed on his shoulders and rolled us over. I straddled him, loving the surprise shining in his wide eyes. With my hands on his rippled chest, my torso straight and my head thrown back, I started moving. Up and down. Rinse and repeat. With each stroke, I went deeper and deeper, taking more of him, filling me up. By all that was sacred, I couldn't get enough of him. Of this.

"Hell," he repeated, letting out a growl.

He closed his hands around my waist and helped me as I went up and down, keeping rhythm with me, taking me even deeper.

I tried focusing, I tried appreciating how hot and handsome he looked under me, but all I could do was whimper with each stroke of him inside me. Drunk with lust, I leaned over him and licked his chest. Gods, how come he was so perfect? Even for a vampire, Drake was too perfect. I grazed my tongue over the ridges of his muscles, trying to memorize them all, but there were so many and I wanted to spend days, weeks, years exploring them all. Then, his muscles tensed under my touch. With a loud growl, he wrapped his hands around my arms and rolled us over again.

"I want you right here," he said, pressing his heavy body over me. I moaned, loving this. I wished this moment would never end.

He captured my mouth with his, kissing me hard as he pounded into me. I moaned again, and my nails clamped on his shoulders, holding on tight.

"By all that is sacred," I mumbled.

Drake increased the rhythm. "You want more?"

"I want it all," I confessed, drunk on him.

He brushed his lips over mine. "You have me. All of me."

He thrust into me once, twice, three more times, and I cried out, coming around him. With another thrust, Drake came too.

His body went limp over me, pressing me against the mattress, his face tucked into my neck, his hot breathing tickling my skin. I felt his fangs as he raked them across my skin, but I wasn't afraid. I wrapped my arms around him, keeping him close, enjoying how we fit together.

Drake licked my neck, then pressed a soft kiss on my skin. He pulled back, just enough to look at me.

"Are you okay?" His fangs were nowhere to be seen.

How he was controlling himself was beyond me, but right

now, I was too satisfied and happy to care. "I told you before, I'm more than okay."

He smiled at me. A real smile that filled my heart with pride.

Slowly, he disentangled himself from me and lay beside me. I felt cold and down from the absence of his body covering mine, but my disappointment was short lived. Not a second later, Drake pulled me to him. He wrapped his arms around me, and I laid my head on his shoulders.

"Sleep now." He kissed my forehead and tightened his grip around me. "I'll keep you safe."

He was gonna keep me safe? He had been the one who was almost killed, and I had just saved him. I knew the healing salve acted fast, but I hadn't expected that well so soon after. I wanted to protest that I could keep myself safe, thank you very much, but his words worked like magic.

Soon, I drifted into a deep sleep.

22

DRAKE

LEAVING THEA ALONE IN MY BED HAD BEEN THE WORST, BUT I had woken up in the middle of the night, thinking of her coven and the heart. As much as I tried to stay in bed with her, to feel her smooth body against mine, run my hands over her silky back, press my nose to her shoulder and neck and let her sweet scent take over me, I felt restless.

The sooner I found out where the heart was, the better. I would retrieve it for her and help her escape. If we were caught, I would fight whoever came for her, while she used her powers to flee—alive and well.

I snuck down the hallways toward Lord Reynard's office. I knew there were patrols instructed to stay close to the door at all times, but I had a plan for that.

Once I was within hearing range—vampire hearing range—but still far from Reynard's office, I pinned a small stash of herbs to the inside of the thick curtains covering a window along a hallway, and with a match, lit them. The herbs released a foul smell, and the fire spread from the herbs to the curtain.

I hid in the shadows of another hallway and waited.

As I expected, the two patrols came to see what the commotion was.

"What a nasty smell!" one said.

"The curtain is on fire!" the other one said.

Like mice in a shoebox, they ran around themselves, trying to pull down the curtains and douse the fire. By the time they figured out what to do, the herbs would be burnt through, and they would investigate how the curtains caught on fire. They would probably wake up Sarki or Alex or Dorian.

In the meantime, I was hoping to have found something useful in Lord Reynard's office.

Once inside, I locked the door and walked to his desk. I lit a small lamp, hoping the dim light wouldn't shine under the door, and started my search.

I knew Reynard had a journal, a diary of sorts—all I had to do was find it. Since Reynard had no reason to believe his office would have been invaded and ransacked, and he certainly didn't think he was going to be murdered the night of the ball, he had no reason to have hidden it, so I started with the obvious places.

His desk, the drawers, the shelves along the walls … then I switched to the less obvious places. In hidden compartments under the desk, or false panels behind the shelves, behind the many painting lining the walls. I even looked under the pool table around the corner.

Nothing.

I sat down on Reynard's chair, leaned back, and racked my mind. Where the hell could his journal be?

I opened the drawer underneath his desk once more. I had already checked in here, but there was nothing more than reports and blank paper and pen in here. But, as I was closing the drawer once more, I realized something: The drawer wasn't deep, and the desk was wide.

I crawled under the desk and sure enough, the panel under the drawer ran the entire width of the desk. I started patting the panel, searching for a lock or something. At the end of the panel, where it met with the wood creating the desk's side panel, there was a lock. A silver circle with an indent of an X. I tilted my head, trying to look at it better. No, not an X. A cross.

I quickly took off my jacket and unpinned the brooch. I threw the jacket over the chair and stared at the cross. Could it be that simple? I guess Lord Reynard didn't need to be too careful if he trusted all of his princes. None of us would ever try something like this while he was alive.

Carefully, I laid the cross flat against the lock.

And nothing happened.

I pressed on it, and nothing happened.

Then, I twisted it ninety degrees.

The popping sound of a lock opening echoed through the office, and one side of the panel swung down. I scooted back and pulled the panel back. And, attached to the top panel of the desk were at least half a dozen journals.

I picked the one I had seen Lord Reynard writing in recently—a thick book-like diary with a leather cover and yellowed pages.

My breathing shallow, I sat back on the chair and flipped through the pages of his journal. First, I searched for the battles against the witches about fifty earlier. As Thea had mentioned, Reynard had wanted to teach the witches a lesson and show them who was actually on top. He attacked the three covens, starting with the Silverblood, and took the heart of the coven.

When he went for the other two covens, most of the witches had run, taking the hearts with them. He vowed to come back and steal their hearts too, but he never did. Not that I knew of.

He mentioned bringing the heart to the castle, showing it off to all of us, then placing it inside a box and hiding it in a secure place. But there was no mention of where.

I skimmed through more pages, stunned by how much he mentioned Sarki—and how unique she was, how powerful she could be, how essential she was to him.

My skin crawled.

I respected Sarki. She was even easy on the eyes, but I had never thought of her like that, and I had no idea why Reynard had fallen so hard for her.

I continued skimming the pages, going from year to year, reading more than I cared to know about the man who had raised me.

Until I stumbled through an interesting entry. A couple of years ago, we had problems with some fae. I remembered the battle that ensued, and when we had won, Reynard took a piece of their crystal tree from them, as a trophy. In this entry, he mentioned "placing the crystal with my other treasures." I flipped through the journal, trying to read more about Reynard's treasures.

I went back over two hundred years, to the beginning of this particular journal, and finally saw it: an entry about Reynard's treasures and the place he kept them all—a hidden stairwell crossing underneath the dungeons that led even farther down below the earth and opened up to a large room.

Hope filled my chest. Even though he hadn't mentioned putting the heart of the Silverblood there once, it was the only place where it could be.

I heard the footsteps coming and put the journal inside the drawer, while pushing the panel underneath up with my knees and closing it once more. Knowing I had no chance of sneaking out without being seen now, I grabbed some of the papers on top of Reynard's desks—reports about the several missions of the couple of weeks before his death, including my little trip to the werewolf packs up north—and pretended to be lost in them.

Prince Albert's scent wafted from under the door before he opened it and walked in.

"I thought I would find you here," he said, closing the door behind him.

My insides stilled. "Why do you say that?"

He raised one eyebrow at me. "Unless I'm mistaken, you set that curtain on fire to take the patrols away from here so you could sneak in without being seen."

Hell ... "Curtains on fire? What are you talking about?"

"Relax," he said, approaching the desk. "I'm on your side, okay? Though, Alex tried buying me yesterday, and I confess the price he was willing to pay was interesting. But I'm not interested. Alex is a jerk and a bully, and he needs to be put down. I'm voting in your favor."

I remembered the voting two days earlier. Prince Albert had voted for me. But it could all be a trap. Alex could have put him up to it, just so I would trust him, tell him about my plans as if I had many, and he would go running to Alex and spill the beans.

If Albert was on my side, I appreciated the vote of confidence, but I preferred being careful at the moment.

"Alex is trying to buy everyone," I said, trying to sound unconcerned.

"He is, and I have to tell you, man, he's promising the world to everyone. He might succeed."

That wasn't good news. "What about you?"

"I don't care. He scares the hell out of me, especially now that he seems intent on taking you out, but I won't let fear win."

I sighed. "You figured out what I was doing. Do you think the others know?"

Albert shook his head. "Nah. I told them I saw a blood slave talking about creating a diversion so he could escape. Alex and Sarki went down to the slave quarters, and I'm guessing it was to interrogate them all."

Hell, I didn't want any blood slave in trouble because of me. "That's good," I lied, feeling sick to my stomach. Knowing Alex, when none of the slaves confessed, he would choose a random one to punish, to make an example out of him.

"Have you found what you were looking for?" Albert asked. I didn't answer. "Because the guards are probably still busy right now. We should leave before they return this way."

I didn't want to take the journal from where I had stashed it, not in front of Albert, so I agreed with him. Together, we walked out of Reynard's office, careful not to make a sound. At the end of the first long hallway, Albert dipped his head at me, then turned to the right, while I turned to the left.

I slowed my steps, and when he turned another corner and disappeared from my sight, I halted. I waited for a minute, to make sure he wasn't coming back and to make sure the patrols weren't coming this way.

Luck wasn't on my side as I sensed new patrols approaching. I had to take a detour and three hallways I didn't really need to, to stay out of the path, then made my way back to Reynard's office.

I needed that damn journal. I had to read it more closely and try to find more clues about that treasure room and where exactly it was located.

As I walked down a hallway, the scent of blood reached my nostrils and my muscles tensed.

Hell, this couldn't be good.

I rushed my steps, following the blood. It got heavier and more distinct the closer I got to it.

No, no, no.

I turned the last corner before Reynard's office doors and halted, my breath lodged in my throat.

Albert was pinned to a wall—a sword in each shoulder and a stake through his heart.

I wouldn't admit it out loud, but finding myself alone in Drake's bed had been like a bucket of cold water that washed away all of my wildest dreams.

After everything we shared last night, he snuck out? From his own bed? Without leaving a note?

What could have happened?

I pushed down the anger threatening to sweep through me and went on with my day. After having done the shortest walk of shame ever—from his bedroom to mine—I took a shower and put on another summer dress and sandals.

I was about to leave my room when Thomas burst in.

"What the he—?"

His eyes were almost the size of his entire forehead. "Prince Drake was arrested."

My heart seized. "What? Why?"

"I don't know yet. I heard someone whispering about it in the kitchen."

"Where is he right now?"

"Last I heard, outside Lord Reynard's office."

"We have to get there."

Thomas frowned. "We shouldn't leave—"

"I don't care!" I shouted. "We have to get to him."

Thomas seemed to consider it for a brief second. Then he said, "Come with me."

Ignoring Drake's warning to not leave his chambers, Thomas and I raced through the corridors. We slowed when we heard voices and movement. The corridor opened up, revealing a dozen vampires arguing in front of heavy double doors.

Prince Alex was there, putting chains around Drake's wrists.

My knees wavered.

As if he had sensed me—or perhaps smelled my scent—Drake's snapped his head and locked his wide eyes on mine. He shook his head once, as if asking me to retreat and leave.

As if ...

I filled my chest with air and marched up to the vampires. "What's going on?"

Alex turned a sly grin toward me. "What do we have here? The traitor's pet. Perhaps she's a traitor too. Should we arrest her?"

Drake snarled, jerking against the heavy chains around his wrists. "Leave her out of this."

"But why? It's so much fun." He glanced at me again. "We could have so much fun."

I ignored his ridiculous advances. "Why are you arresting him? I thought you were still investigating the case."

Another prince stepped to Alex's side and leered at me. "We were, but we caught Prince Drake red handed."

"W-what?"

The prince gestured to the mess behind him.

I gasped as I finally made out what was on the ground. The body of another prince, deep wounds in his shoulders and chest, and dark red blood pooling underneath him. Another one pinned to the wall, but this one hadn't been as lucky as Drake.

I swallowed the bile rising to my throat. "What makes you think Drake did it?"

Another prince started, "Because—"

"We don't owe explanations to a pet," Alex snapped. "If I were you, I would step back before we charge you too."

I clenched my fists, ready to argue more, but when my eyes connected with Drake's, so desolate, so worried, I clamped my mouth shut and stepped back.

Thomas and I stayed to the side, almost out of sight, while Prince Alex laughed his ass off, gloating that he had finally caught the killer and would now avenge his lord.

"What do they mean?" I asked Thomas in a low voice. The vampires could probably hear us, but I didn't care.

"I think ... I think it means Prince Drake is going to be judged and, depending on the sentence, executed."

The air fled my lungs and I had to lean against the wall to stay upright. He couldn't be executed. He wasn't the killer; I was sure of that. But how could I prove it?

Alex and the others dragged Drake down the hallway while Thomas and I watched. I wanted to reach for him, to tell him I would find a way to save him, to tell him how I really felt about him before it was too late.

Drake kept his head high and his gaze straight ahead, but as he walked past me and didn't even glance my way once, a pang cut through my heart.

I knew he was only trying to protect me, but it still hurt.

Thomas had to drag me back to Drake's quarters, because I was too numb to move.

Once Thomas closed the doors behind us, the numbness faded and a current of electricity coursed through me. My muscles trembled and I felt restless.

"We have to do something," I said, pacing the living room.

"I agree, but what?" Thomas wondered. "We're simply blood slaves. Everything we say, every request we make, the princes will laugh at us." He paused, his brow furrowing. "And now that Prince Drake is gone, who knows what will happen to us."

I halted, pointing a finger right at his nose. "Drake isn't gone! Not yet." I sighed and resumed pacing. "There must be something we can do."

I racked my brain for an alternative, but nothing came up. I was a weak witch locked inside a hostile vampire castle. If I dared step foot outside Drake's chambers again, there was no telling what could happen to me. Unless I found out where the heart was and retrieved it, I couldn't see a way to save Drake—or myself.

Tears filled my eyes and, feeling hopeless, I sank on the couch.

"I might have an idea," Thomas said at last.

I perked up, but only a little. I didn't want to hope. "What?"

"It's not about freeing Drake, but I think I can get to him in the dungeons."

I would do anything to see Drake again. "What?"

"I'll be right back." Thomas disappeared through the door leading to the small kitchen. There was a small door there leading to a long and narrow staircase, which wound down to the big kitchen under the castle.

At first, I was stunned Thomas had dropped that bomb then left me to my own thoughts, but while he was gone, I thought about the night before, when Drake had been the one pinned to the wall. Someone had sneaked into his quarters, and if the guards outside hadn't been bribed to let someone come in, then maybe the culprit had come in through the kitchen. I knew there were locks on the door up the stairs and the one at the bottom, but what were locks to a vampire?

I didn't know anymore.

Finally, after an eternity, Thomas came back, panting. "I got it."

I rose to my feet. "You got what?"

"We can get to the dungeons." He beckoned me to follow him. "Come on."

I didn't think twice. Actually, I didn't think at all. I followed Thomas down the dark, winding stairs, my heart racing with anticipation.

"How?" I asked as we went down. I knew he would understand my question.

"The cook likes me, and she has a relationship with one of the dungeon guards," he said. "I remembered her telling me how much her vampire admires Drake and wants him to take over for Lord Reynard. So, I asked her to ask him to let us sneak in."

My heart raced at the prospect of creeping into a dungeon heavily guarded by vampires, but more than that, at the prospect of seeing Drake again.

Pure gratitude filled my chest. "Thank you," I said, my voice breaking.

Thomas stopped and glanced at me, half of his face covered by the shadows in the stairwell. "I confess ... at first, I hated you. You seemed like a spoiled woman who would put my prince in danger. But then, you changed, and he changed." He offered me a half smile. "Despite everything, I think you're bringing our Prince Drake to his full potential." His expression darkened. "Now, if we can find a way of saving him ..."

I didn't answer, because I had no idea how to save him. Right now, my only hope was to find the heart of my coven, but how could I do that if I couldn't—shouldn't—walk around the castle while Drake was imprisoned?

One problem at a time. Right now, I needed to talk to Drake.

Thomas led me to a huge, industrial kitchen with six people—all humans—working and cooking as if there were no tomorrow. One of the cooks, a girl who didn't look much older than I did, approached Thomas and me.

"I'm in the middle of something," she said in a low voice. "Go outside and wait for me. I'll be there as soon as I can."

Without a word, Thomas led me to the hallway outside the kitchen. It was simpler than the rest of the castle, the floor rougher, the walls barer, as if this place wasn't meant for guests.

While waiting, I fidgeted with the straps of my dress, the nervousness in me eating my insides and making me crazy. Thomas didn't look much better as he paced in front of me, biting his nails.

Over half hour later, the girl joined us outside.

"Sorry," she said, her tone still low. "I had to finish a dish before taking a break." She glanced around. "Come with me."

I was probably crazy for following strangers into dark corridors, but what choice did I have? Thomas seemed to trust her, and I knew Drake trusted Thomas. After turning a few corridors and passing a few doors, we followed the human girl down another dark staircase.

She knocked on the thick wooden door at the end of the stairs and waited.

A minute later, the grinding of locks turning echoed around us.

A vampire with pale skin and dark eyes greeted us. "Come quick," he said in hushed tones. "We don't have much time."

Once more, I didn't question it. I only followed.

For all I knew, they could very well be leading me to the dungeons to imprison me, or to some kind of vacant basement, where they could kill me and I would never be found.

Still, I followed them, because they were my only hope of seeing Drake again.

We crossed a long, narrow corridor with many thick wooden doors, reinforced with metal bars, until we halted in front of the last one, at the end of the corridor. This door was even thicker than the others, with more steel bars running across it—vertically and horizontally.

The vampire drew a ring full of keys from his pocket and unlocked the several locks securing the door. He glanced to the other side of the corridor, then at me. "The other guards are patrolling the other levels," he said. "They will be back soon. Be quick."

My heart hammered in my chest when I stepped into the dark, damp cell and magic sizzled around me—this place was reinforced with a witch's magic. The light coming from the half open door behind did little to illuminate the interior, but even I could see Drake kneeling in the back of the cell. Shackles bound his neck, wrists, and ankles to the stone wall.

His shoulders were sagged, his head lolled to his chest. I had never seen Drake like this.

Tears burned the back of my eyes.

Drake lifted his head, his eyes wide, and the light showed me the already healing bruises on his face. "What are you doing here?"

I pushed the tears back down and knelt in front of him. "I had to see you." I cupped his face, careful not to touch any bruise, and he leaned into my palm. "Are you okay? I mean ..."

"I know what you mean," he said. "I'm okay. For now. But it seems someone is trying to either kill me or get me killed by framing me, so I don't think I'll be okay for long."

"What happened? Why were you arrested?"

"I was restless last night and couldn't go back to sleep, so I decided to do something. I went to Reynard's office to search for some clue about where the heart of your coven is hidden."

Pride filled my chest. "Oh, Drake ..."

"Prince Albert found me in the office. He told me Alex is trying to buy the other princes, so they will side with him and I would be charged faster. After talking a little more, we both left the office, but I went back, because I had found something."

I perked up at that. "You did?"

"Reynard kept journals and I found interesting information there, so I went back for the journal, but then I found Albert pinned to the wall right outside Reynard's office."

My hand flew to my mouth. "No ..."

"A second later, guards arrived, followed by Alex and a couple of other princes. They all saw me standing in front of Albert. I was in shock, but Alex was quick to say I had done it."

"And the others believed him."

He nodded. "They did."

I groaned. "Ugh, if I ever find the coven's heart, I'll make sure to teach Alex a lesson."

Drake offered me a weak smile. "I would like to see that." Then, his smile was gone. "In his diary, Reynard doesn't mention where he hid the heart, but he does mention a place where he kept all his treasures. I had planned on reading more of the journal once I had it safe with me back in my chambers, to see if he detailed more of the place and how to get there, but since my plan was derailed ..." He exhaled through his nose.

"But tell me what you know," I urged him. "If I can make sense of it and find the heart, I can restore my power, and then I can come back for you. We'll set things right."

A soft knock on the wall made me jump. "Guards are coming," the vampire guard said. "Let's go."

Drake held my hands in his. "There's a hidden passage underneath the dungeons, a long staircase that leads deep into the earth and to this treasure room. That's all I know." He squeezed my hand. "Please, Thea, be careful."

I leaned into him. "Have some faith in me."

"I do. I don't have faith in the other people living in this castle."

The knock came again. "Hurry!"

Drake tugged my hand and arm until I practically fell on top of him. He pressed his lips to mine, kissing me hard and deep and fast. "Go."

Dizzy from the kiss, I stumbled to my feet. A hand closed around my arm and yanked me out of the cell before I could say a proper goodbye to Drake.

The door closed with a finite thud, and the vampire guard

pulled me into an empty cell in the middle of the hallway. He covered me with a spare blanket that was lying on the dirty ground, its foul scent burning my nostrils, but I understood what he was doing—masking my scent so the other guards wouldn't find me.

Footsteps echoed through the hallway. Once they were faint again, the guard grabbed my arm again and led me out of the dungeons.

"Go now," he whispered.

"Thank you," I whispered back.

He nodded then closed the door between us.

A wave of determination coursed through my veins as I ran back the way I had come. I enjoyed feeling like this, as if I had a plan and could follow it and win. Because there was no other choice. I had to win.

I had felt hopeless before Thea showed up in my cell. Now, I was worried. Because of me, she was about to roam the castle, close to the dungeons, to find the heart of her coven.

If only I could get free and help her, buy her some time.

I jerked against the chains holding me to the wall. I hadn't tried yet, but I was sure I could break free of the chains. However, I could do nothing about the walls and the door. Once the locks fell in, magic enveloped the cell, making it impossible to break through, even with my strength.

A pair of guards unlocked the door and stepped inside the cell. Without a word, they unchained me from the wall and held on to the chains. I wanted to ask where I was being taken, but I didn't want to look curious or worried. Besides, I had a good idea where I was going.

Outside the cell, four guards, all armed with long spears, flanked me. Another four guards joined us outside the dungeons. It seemed the others were worried I was going to attempt to escape if they thought it was necessary to send ten guards to retrieve me.

Ten guards. I glanced at them from the corner of my eyes. They were mostly young vampires, not even a hundred years old. I could easily take down half of them. I might struggle against the other half, but I was sure I could win this round.

Without ceremony, I was pushed in the courtroom, where Sarki, the princes, and half of the vampire residents of the castle were seated in high chairs, looking down at me.

I stood in the middle of what felt like a stage—because everything that was about to happen would certainly be as entertaining as going to the theater. To make the show better, the guards hooked my chains to the stone floor, as if I couldn't break through those either.

My chest trembled, but I forced a lungful of air in, willing my breathing to remain calm. I wouldn't let them see how this bothered me, how I hated being in chains in front of everyone. Up until a few hours ago, most of these vampires looked up to me, and now I was being dragged and tied like a wild animal ready for the butcher.

Dressed in a fine black suit with the silver cross pin secured to the lapel, Alex rose to his feet, a rolled parchment in his hands.

He started his speech formally addressing all the vampires, as he had done many, many times before. The only difference was that never before had a prince stood where I was now.

With long gestures and unnecessary waves of his arms, Alex unrolled the parchment. "Prince Drake DuMoir, you're accused of killing Lord Reynard DuMoir and his personal guards, and Prince Albert DuMoir." I pressed my lips tight before I could bark back. It wouldn't do me any good. He turned to the others, making a big show of it all. "Guards saw Prince Drake entering Lord Reynard's office earlier tonight, followed by Prince Albert. According to the guards, Prince Drake and Prince Albert argued about their plans to take over after having killed Lord Reynard. Apparently, Prince Albert supported Prince Drake at first, but when Prince Albert decided he wanted to take over, Prince Drake retaliated." I clenched my fists and closed my eyes, willing myself to remain calm, to stay cool. "Prince Drake killed Prince Albert the same way he killed Lord Reynard."

Murmurs started around the room. Most of the vampires were hearing the facts for the first time. Hell, I was hearing it all for the first time.

Bastard.

"Is there anything else?" Sarki asked, her voice steady.

Her eyes met mine and I thought I could read what was going on in her mind. If she opened her mouth and told them she had saw me after I was attacked the same way Lord Reynard and Prince Albert had been, I would be quickly discarded as a suspect. But then there would be another problem to worry about: how did I survive the attack? Eventually, the princes would connect the dots and find out about Thea, about how she healed me, and why she was in the castle.

And I couldn't let that happen, and she knew that.

Besides, I doubted Alex would let me off the hook that easily. He would spin another tale in matter of seconds just to incriminate me, no matter what.

"Yes," Alex said, eyeing the parchment. "In fact, we recently learned Prince Drake has been conspiring against Lord Reynard for a few decades."

I snarled. "That's a lie!" I clamped my mouth shut before I said more. If I lost my temper now, things would only get worse.

"Is it?" Alex grinned, a bright, victorious twist of his lips that made me dizzy. "What's all this, then?" One of his lackeys dropped a stack of leather bound books on the table in front of him. Alex picked up the first one. "Look here." He opened the book. Inside, the pages had been swapped with hand-written ones. "These are Prince Drake's journals. He hides them inside normal books so they won't be easily found. But we found them. In these books, Prince Drake describes his hate for Lord Reynard in detail and all of his thwarted plans to kill him over the centuries."

"I never wrote those!" I yelled.

"Then how come it's your handwriting?" Alex asked.

It couldn't be. "I never wrote those," I repeated.

Sarki leaned over the journal and read a page. Her dark eyes widened and she stared at me. "It *is* your handwriting."

I jerked against the chains. "It can't be. I never wrote anything like that!"

"And yet, here it is," Alex said, a triumphant tone to his words. "All the schemes, all the plots, all the failed attempts ... And more. Prince Drake goes into great detail about his love for his human blood slaves, in particular the newest one."

A growl rumbled deep in my chest. "You leave her out of this."

Alex gestured toward me. "See? The mere mention of his latest pet gets him agitated."

I took a long, shaky breath, before continuing. "I don't know how you have my handwriting—magic, perhaps?—but all those entries? I'm sure they are yours. You're the one who took the longest to become a prince out of all of us. You're the one who was always on your knees begging for Lord Reynard's attention. You're the one who always tried to gain advantage over other princes. Perhaps you were tired of groveling and not getting any attention and decided to take action. You killed Lord Reynard so you could become lord of the castle!"

Whispers filled the room.

Something like anger flashed in Alex's eyes before he composed himself and scoffed at me. "And how do you explain Prince Albert's death?"

"You killed him because you saw us talking in Lord Reynard's office. Since you had missed killing me the night before—" Gasps echoed around us. "That's right. Prince Alex invaded my chambers in the middle of the night and pinned me to wall and staked my heart, the same way he did with Lord Reynard and Prince Albert."

"That's a lie!" Alex protested.

"H-how are you alive?" Prince Dorian asked.

"He missed my heart by a mere inch," I explained. "Since he missed killing me, he staged Prince Albert's death to frame me."

"How dare you!" Alex snarled. "Prince Albert was like a brother to me."

"He was afraid of you," I said. "He told me you tried buying him to your side. You even threatened him." I looked out to rest of the vampires in the room. "I bet Prince Alex already bought at least half of you all."

I stared at Gray and Phelps—I knew why they were quiet, why they weren't helping me out here. Because they thought it was all lost. I had lost. And they didn't want to be dragged down with me.

"That's insane!" Alex snapped.

"Prince Drake, you're making serious accusations here," Prince Dorian spoke out, his tone somber.

"It's the truth," I objected. "I didn't kill Lord Reynard or Prince Albert. I would *never* do something like that."

A commotion started on the back of the room and soon a guard rushed forward, something in his hands.

He halted before Alex and Dorian, said something, and handed a small package to them. He bowed, and then returned to his position near the door.

The room was in complete silence as Alex and Dorian examined whatever the guard had handed them.

With stark eyes, Alex fished an item from inside the small leather pouch and lifted it high. A vial with a black liquid. "Vervain mixed with Devil's Touch. Enough to kill a strong vampire."

Vervain? Devil's Touch? The two herbs were rare and hard to secure.

Sarki's brows jumped to her forehead. "Where did you find that?"

"The guards found it hidden in the inside pocket of Prince Drake's jacket."

"That's not mine!" I shouted. Shit. I had forgotten my damn jacket inside Reynard's office. "You took my jacket from Lord Reynard's office after arresting me for Prince Albert's death. You put it there."

Dorian shook his head. "This is too much, Prince Drake. You've gone too far."

"That's not mine!" I raged against the chains, breaking them from the hooks. "Alex is framing me, don't you see?"

Alex pointed a finger at me. "Restrain him!"

In the blink of an eye, the ten guards surrounded me, their spears and swords pointed at my chest. I still thought I could take them, but I couldn't take all of the vampires in the room alone.

I stilled, my breathing shallow.

The whispers were back, louder this time.

"Prince Drake," Dorian spoke up, silencing the room. "You're hereby found guilty for the deaths of Lord Reynard and Prince Albert, and also for plotting to kill other vampires and to take over the castle." He paused. I closed my eyes as if I could avoid hearing the next words. "You'll be executed before dawn."

25

THEA

Back in Drake's quarters, I didn't waste time. I changed from the dress I had been wearing to jeans, a tee, and boots. Next, I picked up the dagger hidden under Drake's pillow and tucked it into my belt. Who knew how easy, or hard, it would be to find this hidden treasure room, and I wasn't naive enough to think I wouldn't run into any vampires while at it. My magic was almost all gone; I couldn't count on it to protect me for long.

Thomas paced around the living room. "What can I do?" he asked for the twentieth time while I finished getting ready.

I had explained to him I needed to find something in order to help Drake, but I hadn't gone into details. The less he knew, the better.

"Just stay here. Keep the doors locked. Hide if you have to." I paused, realizing things could go sideways. "If I can't find what I'm looking for, if Drake ..." I sucked in a sharp breath, because I really didn't want to think about it. "If something happens to Drake, you'll be alone here. You need to find a way to get out of this castle."

His eyes grew big. "B-but … I have nowhere to go."

I placed a hand on his shoulder. "Better lost outside than trapped in here like a slave. Promise me you'll find a way out."

"I-I promise," he said, his voice breaking.

As much as I wanted to believe him, I really doubted he would take any action. If it came down to it, it was more likely Thomas would hide inside Drake's chambers and hope he was left alone, rather than escaping.

If I could, I would have dragged him with me, but I was weak and lost as it was. I couldn't risk taking him down with me.

"Be well," I told him.

"Good luck," he whispered.

My heart hammered as I took the stairs leading to the kitchen. Holy shit, I was going to sneak under the dungeons and try to find a hidden treasure room in a castle swarming with vampires who would rather drain me dry. And I had to hurry because I had no idea what was going on with Drake. I hoped whatever Alex's plans were for him that they would take a while to carry out.

The kitchen was busy, but no human paid much attention to me as I slipped past them.

In the hallway, I held my breath and looked around, straining to hear any sound that would indicate someone was coming. When no sound reached my ears, I started moving, as fast and silent as I could, down the hallway, toward one of the dungeon's entrances.

I was almost at the hidden entrance when I heard a loud growl coming from behind me.

Shit.

I turned and found Prince Alex staring me. First, desire flashed in his eyes, but when his gaze found the dagger hanging at my waist, his eyes darkened. "What do you think you're doing?"

I took a step back, getting closer to the door. Realization hit me. If I went for the door now, he would simply come after me. It would be worse. I had to find a way to get away from him so he wouldn't see where I was headed.

"Answer me, pet!"

I lifted my chin, defiant. I wasn't afraid of him anymore. "I only answer to Prince Drake," I said, knowing it would tick him off.

He let out another deep growl before lunging at me.

With a deep inhale, I summoned the little bit of magic left in me. The power coursed through my veins, warming my insides. I raised my hand and let it out.

A white spark flew from my palm and hit him square in the chest, flinging him back to the other end of the corridor, where he smacked against the archway and hit the stone wall and slid down to the ground.

He groaned, trying to recover. "Guards!" he yelled. I heard heavy footsteps advancing from another hallway. "Get her!" He pointed at me.

I stared at the archway, waiting. After what seemed an eternity, the archway shook, and the stones fell with loud thuds. Smoke filled the hallway.

I didn't wait to see if the guards jumped over the fallen stones and ran through the smoke. I simply spun on my boots and ran. I dashed into the first hidden entrance, cursing under my breath, and praying my plan worked and they didn't see me.

Once the entrance closed behind me, I pulled out a small flashlight Thomas had given me from my pocket and turned it on.

I sucked in a long, steadying breath and moved.

This place was a labyrinth. Long corridors, winding down and down for what felt like forever.

My blood thundered in my ears each time I found more archways, bisected by corridors and stairs. How would I know which way to go? I could only guess and hope I was choosing the right one.

Much like I had done with the hedge maze in the gardens, I marked the way I was going, but this time, I drew tiny arrows on the stone walls every few feet with the dagger I had gotten from Drake.

Hours passed and I didn't feel any closer to where I was supposed to go. And where the hell I was supposed to go? For all I knew, whatever Drake read in Lord Reynard's journal had been lies. False entries so no one could find his beloved treasure room. If it even existed.

But as I was about to take a break, a faint light shone ahead. I hurried my steps, almost tripping down the stairs, until I was standing under a small archway and staring into a wide room that looked like the museum upstairs, though here the items were more obscure: a shelf full of vials with liquids of many colors, another shelf full of books and what looked like journals, pieces of broken furniture taking over a corner, a wall covered by all sorts of weapons and boxes—boxes of every size and shape.

My heart sped up.

This was it. Inside one of these boxes was the heart of my coven.

I had made it.

Eager, I zipped from box to box. Some were too big for the heart, others were too small; I didn't even check them. Others were locked. I groaned each time I tried to open them and couldn't. I would search all of them first, and if I still didn't find the heart, I would go back to the locked ones. I kept going, examining the hundreds of boxes, my hope fading with each false lead.

Until I saw it.

A black box, just the right size, with ancient runes carved around its side. Witch runes.

That was it. This was the box, I was sure of it.

My heart threatened to jump out of my chest as I reached for it. My hands trembled as I tried the lid. To my surprise, I found it unlocked.

I flipped the lid open.

The air fled my lungs.

The box was empty.

26

DRAKE

Hours after being sentenced to death, Alex's men, Ralf and Eden, came into my cell and played piñata with me. They hit me until I bruised and bled. Alex knew I wouldn't dare retaliate now since it would make my situation worse, so he sent his goons to do his dirty work.

Piece of shit.

Later, servants came into my cell, accompanied by guards, and undressed me. They cleaned me with a big, dirty sponge. The quick bath cleaned most of the blood, but it did nothing to close or heal the open wounds. After, they dressed me in all black—shirt, suit, tie, and shoes. They combed my hair and styled the longer strands back with what looked like hair gel. I was ready to attend my own funeral.

When the door opened again over an hour later, I thought it would be Alex to either gloat or take me to my death.

Instead, Sarki strolled in. As usual, she wore a long dark red gown, as if she were going to a party, not the courtroom where I would be killed.

She offered me a warm smile. "Ah, dear Drake."

A thin streak of hope surged up in my chest. "Sarki. You're the oracle. You have influence over the princes. You can help me. Please, make them see I'm innocent. That ... or you have to help me escape."

Her smiled faded, and a new dark shine fell over her eyes. "I can't do that, Drake."

"But I thought you wanted me to take Lord Reynard's place."

"I did, but things have gone sideways. You see, when I killed Reynard—" My breath caught. "—I was hoping to incriminate that insufferable Alex, but unfortunately, things spun out of my control and you're taking his place."

"W-what? You killed Lord Reynard?" It didn't make sense. She had loved him. "But why?"

"Because I'm tired of just sitting on the sidelines and only be useful when visions come to me. For centuries, I've been standing here and looking pretty, when in fact I'm more powerful than you all!"

I shook my head. "This is crazy, Sarki. Please, tell me you're joking."

Her brows slammed down, and a ripple of her power rushed over me like an electric wave. I shuddered. "Reynard was a monster. A monster I had to pretend to love and look up to. I would have killed him long ago, if I had had the chance."

"He wasn't a monster ..."

"He was! He killed your family! He killed my mother! He abducted me and raised me against my will! He kept me as a prisoner until I learned to behave! He didn't care about anyone, only power." She snorted. "Where's his power now?"

Usually, I was quiet because that was me. I was a quiet

man. But right now? Right now, I was speechless. I wanted to rage, to yell, to yank those chains and tie them around this half-witch's neck and make her pay for having killed Lord Reynard and starting this huge mess.

My breath caught as I realized something. "What about me? Did you try to kill me?"

"No," she said, sounding less crazy, less enraged. "I really like you, Drake. More than you'll ever know. I wouldn't have killed you. I think that was Alex, for once, trying to take advantage of the situation."

"And Albert?"

"That *was* me, though you weren't supposed to go back to Reynard's office. I knew Alex was close by, and I wanted to draw him there and frame him instead." She sighed as if annoyed with how I messed up her plans. She was insane. "But now there's nothing I can do to save you. Unless ..."

"What?" I asked. I would accept almost anything that could save right now. Almost. "Unless what?"

She approached me, strolling like a cat on the prowl. "Take me as your mate. If you do, then I'll help you kill Alex and any other prince who opposes us, and we can rule Castle DuMoir together."

I stared at her in horror and shock that she would suggest something like that. Or worse, that she thought I would accept her offer. "Never."

She put her hand on her hips. "Is that because of your little pet? Are you in love with her?" I pressed my mouth tight, but my silence was answer enough. She gasped. "You are! You love her."

"That's none of your business," I said with a bite.

"Oh, but it is." She tilted her head. "One last chance to change your mind. Forget Thea and be my mate."

"Never," I snarled the word this time.

She tsked. "Then I have no choice but to kill Thea." My blood became ice. "I'll see you again before your execution to let you know your pet is dead."

With a flip of her hair, Sarki spun around and sashayed out of my cell. The door closed with a loud thud, followed by the clicks of the locks falling into place.

I roared, jerking against the chains and breaking them once more.

I punched the walls and the doors, but with the magic imbued in them, they didn't even budge, didn't even make a sound.

With bloody fists, I knelt on the floor and screamed my rage and my frustration away.

I STARED AT THE OPEN BOX, THE RED VELVET LINING MARKED BY the heavy weight of something that wasn't there anymore.

The heart. Where was the damn heart?

I continued my previous task, opening all the boxes I could and searching for the heart, even though I knew, I felt, the damn heart had been in that other box—not long ago.

By all sacred things. This couldn't be happening. It was so, so close, and yet so far away. Where could the damn heart be?

Tears sprang to my eyes, but I pushed them down. I didn't have time for despair. If I couldn't find the heart, then I had to change tactics. Change objectives. Change quests. Damn my powers. I would have to save Drake with or without them.

I picked up Drake's dagger and held it tight. I wasn't the best fighter, but it was all I had.

Taking a deep breath, I turned to leave the room.

And froze.

Sarki walked into the room.

"Sarki?" I asked, taking a few steps toward her. "What happened? Where's Drake?" Another thought came into my mind. "What are you doing here?"

She crept up to me, moving her hips more than necessary, a smile spreading over her red lips. "I'm here to take care of unfinished business."

"What?" I gasped, sensing great power coming from her. How hadn't I felt it before? I stared at her chest, stunned. "You have the heart."

"Finally!" she spread her arms, as if present a big award. "Yes, the heart of your coven beats in my chest."

I took a step back. "When did you figure it out?"

"That you came for the heart? I wasn't sure at first, but after you healed Drake, I did some digging. It wasn't easy." She placed her hand over her heart. "But I'm powerful, you know."

I frowned. "If you're powerful, then why didn't you heal Drake?"

"Why would I heal someone I was trying to get rid of?"

"You ... you tried to kill Drake?" Realization dawned on me. "Y-you killed Lord Reynard," I whispered, more appalled by the second.

"And I can honestly say I enjoyed it. Shame it was so fast."

"This doesn't make sense." I shook my head. "I thought you liked Drake."

She tsked. "Drake was my favorite. I never wanted anything bad to happen to him. But he got in my way and started digging too deep. Soon, he would find out what I had done and I couldn't let that happen, even if it pained me."

I stared at her, disgusted. "You're insane."

She shrugged. "One does what one must."

I didn't care about Sarki's reasons. I didn't care that she tried to kill Drake. I didn't care about any of it. As long as she gave me the heart and I could rescue Drake, she could do whatever she wanted.

I pointed the dagger at her. "Give me the heart."

She tilted her head. "I can't do that."

"I don't care! Give me the damn heart!"

Sarki picked up the black box and turned it around her hands, as if examining the engravings along the sides. "You see, I'm the rare offspring of a witch and a vampire." Very rare indeed. Ninety-nine percent of vampires were sterile and witches didn't conceive easily. "Everyone thought Reynard was my lover, but that was a decoy. I was his daughter. The bastard stole me from my mother and then killed her just because. I hated the man with all my heart, but I was weak. There was nothing I could do against him. If he wanted, he could have killed me in less than a second. But he didn't. He took care of me, even when I tried to rebel."

"Stop!" I cried. I wasn't going to sympathize with her, even if I did feel sorry for her. Like Drake, her family had been killed by Reynard and she had been taken by force.

She went on. "There aren't many half-witches, half-vampires out there, so not everyone knows we are weak. The two kinds of blood don't mix well. They are practically incompatible, actually. With the passing of the years, we found out I was dying. Then, when Reynard came across your coven and stole the heart, he had the idea of giving it to me." She pointed to her chest. "I had a hard adaptation period, let me tell you, but I made it. And, to my surprise, it worked. Suddenly, I was strong, well, and powerful. So, so powerful." She raised her hand and a blue flame appeared in her palm. "Unfortunately, I can't live without the heart, and I know you're after the heart, so I'm afraid you'll have to die."

She threw the blue flame at me.

I ducked behind a pile of boxes. The flame exploded, breaking several of the boxes, and sending me to my butt.

Panting, I crawled back, hiding behind some low stone pillars. I needed a minute, a second, to come up with a plan. How would I fight against a witch with the power from my coven's heart?

"Come out, come out, wherever you are," she teased, her voice echoing throughout the room, making it impossible to know where she was, or how close she was.

Damn it.

She was a witch and a vampire. She could use her powers and her strength and speed on me. I was doomed.

But I couldn't be doomed.

I was this close to getting my coven's heart back, in succeeding in my suicide mission, and in saving Drake. I wouldn't be doomed.

I remembered the other shelves in this room, filled with many things. I could—

A blue flame zipped past the pillar, its heat singeing my ear.

Shit.

"There you are!" Sarki said, jumping in front of me.

She raised her hand, showing off a new blue flame.

Fast, I scooted closer and, grunting, did a low sweeping kick. Not expecting such a move from me, Sarki tripped and fell.

I lifted the dagger high, ready to stab her.

A scream echoed through the room as Sarki summoned a huge blue flame and hurled it at me.

I took off running. The flame exploded on a pile of boxes, sending splinters flying everywhere. A thick splinter pricked my upper arm, and I groaned but didn't stop.

Dodging boxes, pillars, and shelves for cover, I reached the shelf with the vials. As quickly as I could, I read the labels while ducking from incoming flames. I found a couple of poisons, but they all had to be administered by drinking a large quantity. Finally, I found something useful and—

A force surrounded me, and suddenly, I couldn't move.

"I'm tired of this game," Sarki said. The force—her power—turned me around. Grinning, Sarki flung her hand, and I rushed backward. My back hit the wall behind me, taking my breath away. "You're going to die now, little pet, and I'll enjoy every second of it."

The force pressed me against the wall, as if she were trying to squash me like a bug. My muscles groaned, my arms stretched, my head burned, my lungs collapsed. I couldn't breathe, my vision blurred, my arms went numb, and despair gripped inside me.

No, no, no, this couldn't be the end.

It wouldn't be the end.

Fighting against the force, I turned my hand, just a tiny bit, and then threw the vial at her. "Eat this, bitch," I spat.

It exploded and a violent tornado-like wind escaped. Sarki was flung back, and I fell on the floor, released from her magic.

My knees screamed from hitting the floor, my lungs hurt from breathing too deep, my head spun, but I had to push through. I had to move.

Focusing on one thing only, I charged at Sarki.

I stepped into her space and plunged the dagger in her gut. Sarki's eyes went wide, her mouth fell open, and she curled into me. She gasped for air as blood seeped from her wound.

"I'm sorry," I whispered, pulling the dagger out. The dust of witch's bark on the blade was now covered with her blood. The herb, which I had snatched from the night we had healed Drake, acted fast. My coven used it primarily to relax a witch with deep wounds, so she would let us work on her without lashing out. But when used in greater quantities, it could numb a witch for a couple of hours.

I didn't know the effects it would have on a half-witch, half-vampire, but judging by the way Sarki's body went limp against mine, I would say it worked well enough.

I helped her to the floor, laying her flat against the cold stone. Even with the witch's bark, she was able to move a little. She pressed a hand to her wound, but I had gone for the right place. Blood flowed from between her fingers and created a crimson pool around her shaking body.

Her eyes rolled back and she gasped, as if trying to say something.

Disgusted with myself, I placed a hand over her mouth and nose. I wished I could give her an honorable death, but I didn't have time to waste. All the vampires were probably looking for me, and Drake needed help ASAP.

Sarki jerked against my hold, but the strength left her. Not long after, she went slack.

A sob ripped through my chest as I lifted the dagger again and aimed for her chest.

Thinking of the future of my coven and saving Drake, I opened up Sarki's chest and carved out my coven's heart. The moment I held it in my bloodied, trembling hands, power surged into me.

I gasped and tilted my head back as I took in the power, as I let it flood me, fill my veins and my own heart.

My mind revolved, my heart pounded, my veins, not used to this magnitude of power, thrummed.

When my body recovered, I tucked the heart into my little purse and shot to my feet.

Now I was ready to save a certain vampire.

DRAKE

I KNEW IT WAS CLOSE TO DAWN WHEN THE GUARDS OPENED THE doors of my cell.

Sarki hadn't come back. Thea hadn't come. What the hell happened to them? I felt sick thinking that Sarki could have gotten to Thea, and only hell knew what the sick woman could have done.

A sea of guards entered the dungeon cell. Two of them unhooked my chains from the wall and held them tight, while the others kept their spears pointed at me.

While they dragged me back to the courtroom, the thought of fighting them crossed my mind several times. I analyzed everything. As we crossed the wide corridor leading to the main floor, I imagined running through there. Then the stairs leading to the main foyer. I even imagined myself breaking down the big crystal chandelier outside the ball-room as a distraction.

But it was no use. I would never make it outside, not with the quantity of vampires living in the castle.

So, like an obedient puppy, I walked with the guards to the courtroom. As expected, the place was full, even more than during my judgment. Almost all vampires, save for a few guards patrolling the castle, were probably here.

Seated in a privileged spot along with the other princes, Alex looked particularly gleeful. His eyes shone as he stared down at me.

A wooden platform holding the sharp-looking guillotine had been brought to the center of the courtroom. I hadn't seen this in decades. Maybe even over a century.

And now I was going to die in it.

I was pushed to the platform and brought down to my knees in front of the guillotine.

Grinning, Alex walked up to the platform, followed by Dorian.

"Prince Drake," Dorian started. "You've been sentence to death for the murder of Lord Reynard and Prince Albert. Any last words?"

"Yes," I said. "When Thea comes to kill you all, tell her I love her."

A commotion started in the crowd and whispers rose to chatter. Killing? Thea? The blood slave? They had no idea what I was talking about.

"Silence!" Dorian shouted.

Instantly, the chatter died.

Alex leaned into the platform and said, "Your little blood slave attacked me earlier. I have the full force of the guards after her. She won't be able to do a thing. Besides, you don't have to worry about her." He grinned at me. My spine chilled. "I plan on taking good care of her."

I jerked against my chains, wishing I could squeeze his

neck a little before I was executed. Perhaps I could even kill him. Since I was about to die anyway, I wouldn't feel too bad about it.

The guards pushed my torso down over the bottom of the guillotine, and then they closed it around my neck. Like the chains, I could easily break out of here, but there was no point in that.

I could only pray to whatever god was listening that Thea found the heart and made it out of the castle before the vampires got to her.

Accepting my fate, I closed my eyes.

The sound of the blade coming down and cutting the air echoed in my ears.

Magic whipped across the room, an electrical charge like lightning. The blade flew several feet away, slicing a guard in half, and the wood around me exploded into millions of splinters.

I looked up and found the entire room frozen, staring at the woman standing at the door, her hand stretched in front of her.

"Thea," I whispered. My chest tightened.

"Kill her!" Alex shouted.

The room erupted into chaos.

Every vampire turned to Thea. Pride filled my veins as I watched the vampires coming at her and Thea flinging them off with a simple wave of her hand, one by one.

Her clothes and hands were bloodied, and dark circles stained the skin under her eyes, but she looked powerful, fierce, stunning. As if she were Moses parting the Red Sea, Thea pushed the vampires away with her power, opening a path to the center of the room. To me.

Waking up from my stupor, I broke free of the rest of the chains. A guard noticed what I was doing and turned to me. A second later, my dagger zoomed past me and pierced his heart. I glanced over my shoulder, but Thea was busy with the others.

I grabbed my dagger from the vampire's chest. His body fell on the platform. The dagger hadn't killed him, but he would be out for a little while.

Holding my dagger tight, I made my way to Thea. Too worried about the witch in the room, the vampires had forgotten about me. I took advantage of my element of surprise and advanced on them. I sliced their necks or pierced their heart from behind, taking them out in a second and putting them out of commission for the rest of the night.

The other princes were the only ones holding their own against Thea. They advanced on her, she pushed them back, but unlike the others, they lunged at her a moment later.

Finally, I reached her. I stood beside her, my dagger in hand, ready to stab the vampires or rip their throats out.

I was undone when Thea took the dagger from me, pulled my back into her chest, and held the dagger against my neck.

"Stay back or he dies!" she shouted, retreating to the back of the room.

Laughing, Alex stepped forward. "You can kill him. We don't care."

"What are you doing?" I whispered, careful so the other vampires couldn't hear it.

"Just play along," she whispered back. Then she raised her voice and asked, "So you don't care about the truth? What if I tell you Sarki is responsible for killing Lord Reynard and Prince Albert?"

The princes stared at her as if she were crazy. "It's the truth. She let Drake take the blame, since it would be easier for her."

"Easier for her to do what?" Nolan asked.

"To take over the castle and rule you all."

Alex let out a loud, incredulous laugh. "You think we'd believe that?"

Thea pushed me down. Her strength was pathetic, but since I was playing along, I let her. I fell on my knees. Next, she used my dagger and sliced her palm. Blood dripped on the floor while she whispered words. An image, like a hologram appeared in front of us.

It was Sarki and Thea in a strange room.

Thea pointed my dagger to Sarki, who seemed unfazed.

"You ... you tried to kill Drake?" Thea asked in a whisper. "Y-you killed Lord Reynard."

"And I can honestly say I enjoyed it. Shame it was so fast."

"This doesn't make sense." Thea shook her head. "I thought you liked Drake."

Sarki tsked. "Drake was my favorite. I never wanted anything bad to happen to him. But he got in my way and started digging too deep. Soon, he would find out what I had done and I couldn't let that happen, even if it pained me."

"You're insane," Thea said.

She shrugged. "One does what one must."

"That's all magic," Alex shouted, turning toward her. "You're changing it."

Nolan shook his head. "I've seen this before. This is blood magic and it can't be altered." He turned to the other vampires. "This witch is showing us the truth."

"Where's Sarki?" Gray asked.

The image faded away.

"I killed her," she admitted.

Alex growled. "You attacked me earlier today, you revealed Sarki was the one behind the killings, and now you're telling us you killed her. Very convenient, don't you think?"

"But the blood magic—"

"Could be another lie!" Alex shouted, interrupting Nolan. "Theatrics. She's pretending to use blood magic while she shows us an illusion." A few other princes nodded. "I say we need clarification." He pointed at her. "Get her!"

Thea flung her hand and the princes flew to the far wall. Swords were drawn from various bodies on the floor. They soared toward the princes, piercing their shoulders and pinning them to the wall, several feet from the ground.

They growled, howled, shouted, jerked against the swords, but didn't move.

"Get her!" Alex shouted again.

The remaining vampires turned on us, their fangs bared, their hands in claws. The ones with swords and weapons pointed them at us.

"What now?" I asked.

Thea waved her hand and a translucent blue wall appeared between the vampires and us. She quickly grabbed my arm and pulled me up to stand beside her. She pressed the dagger to my neck again.

Still holding on to me, Thea retreated to the back door. Once we were past it and away from all eyes, she lowered the dagger and stepped into me.

"I thought I lost you," she said, her voice breaking.

I embraced her. "And I thought I had lost you." I buried my face on her neck. "I'm glad you're okay."

Shouts came from the courtroom.

"The shield won't hold for long." She slipped her hand into mine. "Let's go."

Together, we ran out of the castle. Together, we were free.

I DIDN'T KNOW THE WOODS AROUND THE CASTLE, BUT DRAKE did. Using his super speed and my magic, we practically flew across the woods, getting as far away from the castle as we could. We even ran past Crimson Glen, and kept going for hours, afraid that, if we stopped, the princes would catch up with us.

Finally, we came across an empty cottage high in the mountains and decided to stop to clean up and rest. While Drake scouted the perimeter to make sure no one had followed us, I cast a protective shield in a five-mile radius using the power from my coven's heart.

Together, we stumbled inside the small and cozy cottage. By the looks of it, its owners hadn't been here recently. There were clean dishes on the counter, folded linens on the couch, and the pantry was full of food.

I helped Drake to the sofa, dropped the bag with the heart on the small coffee table, and knelt beside him. "How long since you last drank blood?"

He groaned, leaning back. None of his wounds looked too

bad, but after spending the night in the dungeon suffering at Alex's hands, fighting our way out, and running for hours, he was certainly spent. "I don't know. Over twenty-four hours, I think."

Damn it. I rolled the sleeve of my shirt up and offered him my wrist. "Here."

He pushed my arm away. "I won't drink from you."

"You have to," I insisted. "Or you'll have to hunt for some animal outside and you're too weak for that."

"But if I take from you, you'll be weak."

I shook my head. "I have magic, and if I need sustenance, I can cook something for myself." He locked his dark green eyes on mine. So pained, so raw. The shine in them twisted my gut. "Please," I whispered.

He took my arm and leaned over me. I sucked in a sharp breath, getting ready for the prickle of his fangs, but instead he planted a soft kiss on my wrist.

"I have a better idea," he said, his voice low. He rose, pulling me with him, then gently pushed me back until I hit the wall across the room. Drake hooked his fingers under the hem of my shirt and tugged it over my head. He lowered his mouth to my shoulder and rained kisses on my skin, making my breathing grow shallow. My stomach tensed as his lips made their way up my neck as his hands clasped around my waist. "Relax," he whispered, his breath hot against my skin.

I exhaled, but that did little to ease the anticipation growing in me. "Just get on with it." I wasn't afraid of his bite, not really, but I confess I wasn't looking forward to it either.

Drake looked into my eyes. "Thea ... thank you."

I tilted my head. "I didn't do anything."

"You did. You saved me from myself. From them."

I stood on tiptoes and stretched my neck so my lips were

only half an inch from his. "I think you're dizzy and mumbling nonsense."

One corner of his lips curled up before he dipped into me and captured my lips. His tongue ravished my mouth and his hands snaked around my bare midriff. With deft fingers, he unclasped my bra. What the hell was he doing? He had to drink my blood before we did anything else.

I pulled back a little to voice my concerns, but gasped when Drake spun me around. He pressed his chest on my back, his hips on my ass—and I felt his erection. With a groan, he cupped my hips and made his way up, until his palms closed around my breasts. Despite myself, I wiggled my hips, brushing more of me against him. Finally, he pushed my long hair to the side, and I turned my head at an angle, giving him full access to my skin. His hands returned to my breasts and he leaned into my neck. He brushed his lips over my skin, drawing a shiver from me, and then bit down. I let out half a cry, half a moan.

Pure ecstasy flooded me, and when Drake pinched my nipples, I cried again. I was drowning. I was losing it. I was in damn heaven.

I moved my hips, drawing a growl from him. I clasped one of his hands and guided it down, from my breast, down to my belly, and inside my pants.

Knowing exactly what I wanted, Drake pushed his hand under my panties and brushed a finger over my clit. The mix of his touch, his bite, my feelings for him ... it was too much. I melted. Needing some other support, I splayed my hands on the wall before me.

Slowly drinking from me, Drake slipped a finger inside me, while rubbing my clit with his thumb and pinching my nipple with his other hand.

"By all the sacred things," I mumbled.

He thrust another finger inside me and pushed them deeper. Surprising me, he retreated his fangs and licked my neck. Then his mouth was over my ear. "Thank you, my love."

My love ...

His words resonated in me, and as if by magic, I climaxed, exploding in his arms.

Slowly, he slipped his fingers from me and turned me around. He leaned over me and pulled my pants all the way down. He made quick work of getting rid of his clothes, and without giving me a chance to stare at his incredible physique, he pressed against me again. He ran his hands down my hips, and on instinct, I wound my legs around his waist. He trapped me between the wall and his hard, hard body. His hands cupped my ass as he positioned my hips right on his, so I could feel how aroused he was. Heat spread through me, and I moaned from the pure bliss of knowing I made him like that.

Gently, he slid inside me.

His hands on my hips, Drake closed his eyes and growled. "Hell ..." He leaned into me and mashed his mouth against mine, taking me for a deep and very, very slow kiss, matching the pace he was moving inside me.

It was too much, but still not enough. I needed more of him; I needed all of him. As much as I could, I lifted my hips and met him halfway, increasing the rhythm, taking him even deeper.

Drake bit down on my lower lip and groaned. "Thea..." It sounded like a warning, but I didn't care, I had to keep moving. After almost losing him, I didn't care about anything else. Just him and me. Us.

Nothing else mattered.

He placed a kiss on my neck, where he had bitten me, then his tongue trailed down, around the curve of my breast, before dipping down some more. A shiver ran up my spine when he closed his mouth around my nipple.

Crying out, I arched my back and my hands gripped his hair. He lapped his tongue around my nipple and sucked on my breasts, still pumping into me, each stroke faster and deeper than the last.

The fire took me over and I drowned in flames. I cried his name as I came. Drake sucked on my nipple one last time before pulling back and staring into my eyes. "I love you, Thea," he groaned.

Surprised, I gasped, and before I could say anything, his mouth fell over mine. Our tongues dueled, asking, demanding everything. He thrust one, two, three times ... and then he growled and clutched me to him, his body quivering against mine.

I wound my arms around him and held him tight. A deep, raw emotion filled my chest, and I whispered in his ear, "I love you too."

I watched Thea while she slept in my arms, recovering from the ordeal of the last thirty hours. After spending the night in the dungeons, getting beaten up, fighting with my coven, running away, and making love to this beautiful woman, I was exhausted too. But no matter what I did, I couldn't sleep.

My mind was too busy, my soul unrested.

As much as I would like to send everything to hell and run away with Thea, that wasn't the solution. Thea had to at least stop by her coven and hand them the heart before leaving with me. But witches were greedy old things, most of them, and I was sure they wouldn't let her go that easily. Sacrificing herself for the mission? Just fine. Running away with a vampire? It was a declaration of war.

No matter where we hid, my coven and her coven would come after us, and they would find us. We would never have any peace.

Unless ... we did it right. Unless, we took it upon ourselves to avoid the oncoming war and bring peace to all races from the inside. It would be hard, it would take time, but I believed we could do it.

Inhaling deeply, I ran a hand down Thea's cheek. After tasting her blood, her scent had become even stronger to me, more potent. I had been crazy about her scent before. Now? I didn't think there was a word to explain what I felt right now.

But I could push down the hunger for her sweet, sweet blood, because I had found out something else: I loved her. With all my soul and my dead heart, I loved her. I could endure being by her side as long as she let me love her.

I brushed my fingers over her neck, right where I had bitten her, and she squirmed in my arms, pressing more of her long legs on mine.

This woman, this beautiful woman, had freely offered her blood to save a vampire. Witches hated vampires, just as vampires hated witches, but this beautiful woman hadn't hesitated. She let me have her blood, and her body, and then she handed me her heart too.

When she had said she loved me too, I was sure I had gone to heaven.

Though, I didn't deserve heaven. I didn't deserve this woman.

But maybe, if I went back and fixed things, if I went back and reformed my coven, I could try to be worthy of her.

I sucked in a sharp breath when a new thought came to mind: Thomas was still there, alone in the castle with many hungry and angry vampires.

Hell.

Thea moved again. "Why are you awake?" she whispered, her eyes closed.

"How do you know I'm awake?"

"I can hear the wheels inside your head turning."

I snorted. "Right. As far as I know, witches don't have acute hearing."

"Nope, but some of us have a pretty good sixth sense." Her eyes fluttered open. She shifted some more, resting her chin on my chest and starting me with those two gray marbles. "The heart is giving me too much power right now. I can sense everything from miles away."

I ran my hands down her naked back. "Really? What are you sensing right now?"

"Two miles west, I sense two deer who are unaware of the wolf watching them, waiting for the right time to attack. I sense a flock of birds that keep jumping from tree to tree. I sense a handful of rabbits in their burrows, a few snakes slithering by, some spiders, and a lot of nasty bugs." She wrinkled her nose. "But no humans. Though, I sense a vampire whose body is too tense after having a relaxing night."

Chuckling, I kissed the top of her head. "It was a good night indeed."

"But ..."

How could this woman, this wonderful woman, know me so well? I sighed. "But ... I think we have to go back." Her body tightened under my touch. "You to your coven, and me to mine."

Thea withdrew from me, a question in her eyes, so I sat up and held her arms and kept her close while I explained all that had been on my mind the past couple of hours. She didn't say a single word, while I went on and on, hoping she would understand my logic.

After a long moment of silence, she nodded. "I know you're right, but I still don't like it."

"I don't like it either." I squeezed her hands in mine. "I don't want to leave you."

"But you will." She sighed. "Even if I disagree with your plan, I can see your mind is already made up."

I pulled her even closer, until she sat on my lap, and I looked deeply into her eyes. "There's nothing I want more than to be with you. Hell, I had never wanted anything until you came into my life. Now, I want you and I won't let go. Never. But before we can be together and in peace, we have a big mess to clean up." I rested my forehead to hers, trying to memorize it all. Her scent, her warm, soft skin, her shiny gray eyes, her plump lips, and her wonderful body. I wanted to engrave them into my memory—how she felt against me, how we fit together, how powerful she made me feel. "Do you trust me?"

She wound her arms around me, and even though she tried to hide it, I could hear her rapid heartbeat and how her breathing hitched, as if she were fighting back tears. "I do," she whispered.

Taken aback by her emotions, I leaned into her and captured her mouth with mine. I couldn't stop myself, and soon we were back in each other's arms, our bodies tangled together as we made love one more time.

Afterward, we got dressed and Thea had a quick breakfast. She insisted I drink more of her blood before I passed out, but I assured her that once I was back at DuMoir Castle, I would drink a handful of bottles of blood to make sure I would be okay.

Holding hands, we walked out of the cottage and to the edge of Thea's invisible shield.

I snaked my arms around her, pressed her body against mine, and claimed her lips once more. After savoring her taste, after I was sure I wouldn't forget it, I pulled back, enough to look into her eyes. "I promise you that we'll be together again."

Her nails sank into my shoulders. "I'll hold you to that promise."

I pressed my lips to her forehead. "Be well, my love."

Thea sniffed. "And you be careful."

Leaving her was harder than I thought it would be, especially when she was so shaken by it. If I didn't leave now, I wasn't so sure I would.

Channeling my courage, I brushed my lips on hers once more, then spun around and ran.

For the first two miles, I could hear Thea's soft sobs. It was hard to keep going when all I wanted was to go back and embrace her one more time. And then I wasn't so sure I could ever leave her again.

So I kept going, kept running, while the promise I made to her echoed in my mind.

We'll be together again.

CONTINUE READING ABOUT THEA AND DRAKE ON BOOK 2, *THE WITCH QUEEN*.

THANK YOU

Thank you for reading *The Vampire Heir*!

Reviews are very important for authors. If you liked my book, please consider leaving a review on your favorite vendor and/or on goodreads, please!

Grab book 2 of the series, *The Witch Queen*, now!

Don't forget to sign up for my Newsletter to find out about new releases, cover reveals, giveaways, and more!

If you want to see exclusive teasers, help me decide on covers, read excerpts, talk about books, etc, join my reader group on Facebook: Juliana's Club!

ABOUT THE AUTHOR

While USA Today Bestselling Author Juliana Haygert dreams of being Wonder Woman, Buffy, or a blood elf shadow priest, she settles for the less exciting—but equally gratifying—life as a wife, a mother, and an author. She resides in North Carolina and spends her days writing about kick-ass heroines and the heroes who drive them crazy.

Subscribe to her mailing list to receive emails of announcement, events, and other fun stuff related to her writing and her books: www.bit.ly/JuHNL

For more information:
www.julianahaygert.com

facebook.com/julianahaygert
twitter.com/juliana_haygert

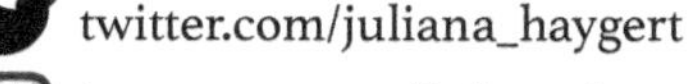
instagram.com/juliana.haygert

The Blood Pact (Book 9)

The Fire Heart Chronicles
Heart Seeker (Book 1)

Flame Caster (Book 2)

Sorrow Bringer (Book 3)

Earth Shaker (Novella)

Soul Wanderer (Book 4)

Fate Summoner (Book 5)

War Maiden (Book 6)

The Everlast Series
Destiny Gift (Book 1)

Soul Oath (Book 2)

Cup of Life (Book 3)

Everlasting Circle (Book 4)

Willow Harbor Series
Hunter's Revenge (Book 3)

Siren's Song (Book 5)

Breaking Series
Breaking Free (Book 1)

Breaking Away (Book 2)

Breaking Through (Book 3)

Breaking Down (Book 4)